THE WAY KNIGHT

A TALE OF REVENGE AND REVOLUTION

ALEXANDER WALLIS

Cover art by Phil Ives

Illustrations by Anastasia Ilicheva

ISBN-13: 978-0-9929899-4-1
ISBN-10: 0992989949

For all the young people it has been my privilege to work with.

Fare well on your journeys.

To Catherine,
Fare well on your journey,
Alex Wallis

CONTENTS

Act One – The Traitor

Act Two – The Way Knight

Act Three – The Great Mother

Appendices

ACT ONE

THE TRAITOR

The Traitor

Now she knew with absolute certainty. She was the Goddess of War. She was the avenger, chaos and death. She was Cere-Thalatte and the falling stars were a measure of her anger.

As the heavenly fire descended, she raised her sword, light flashing on the bloody tip. Shadows took life and prowled the battleground, delineating the abundant dead. The Goddess had repaid greed with slaughter; a thousand lives shed for one.

As the screaming stars rained down, her laughter became a haunting song.

I am the crown of eternal stars,
I am the armour forged from scars,
I am the truth whose seed is doubt,
I am the flaming sword that will never burn out!

The song was carried to its conclusion by the theatrical players as the battleground became a stage and the stage little more than a hill upon which they had practised their craft. Falling stars became wooden torches. Bodies rose happily from the dead. Masks of virtue and vice were cast aside to reveal the cheery grins of actors. Having concluded their performance, the players bowed to the gathered villagers of Jaromir.

Daimonia Vornir led the applause with all her heart. She had been so completely absorbed in the drama that she came back to herself with a jolt. She was no longer the heroine of the mythological saga but merely a wide-eyed girl cheering into the wind.

'Goddess, give me your certainty,' Daimonia prayed, 'for I am beset with questions and doubt.' She blinked a swell of tears, her heart tired from the demands of the drama.

Others were unmoved by the play. Daimonia's older brother, Niklos Vornir, sat with arms folded tightly across his surcoat, forbidding his hands to clap.

'What was it all for?' Niklos complained, making a sneer of his pretty face. He had noble but narrow features like their grandfather Jhonan. 'Why did they fight and struggle and love if it all came to nothing?'

'Are flowers less beautiful because they die?' Daimonia laughed. She had dark hair and large insistent eyes like their mother. It was a face that was strong and earnest, but something about the cusp of her lips suggested an unanswered question.

Niklos had already lost interest. He noticed some of the village wives watching him fondly and pride reddened his cheeks. In Jaromir children were raised by the whole community, each adult considering themselves shareholders in the upbringing of healthy useful children. Niklos was now a Knight of the Accord, a prestigious honour even for a child of knights. Visiting his childhood home as a noble was an act of respect and gratitude.

'Tonight I'll sleep in my old room in Vornir Manor,' Niklos told his sister. 'And we'll again share secrets by the fire.'

Daimonia allowed herself a childish excitement at the proposition. She clung to Niklos' arm, surprising him with her intensity. His return was a light banishing all her lonely and disturbing thoughts. He was the sum of all her best memories, his presence like many days poured into one.

Niklos acted like a man seized by the militants. He struggled with his posture as Daimonia swung on his arm, battling to maintain his knightly bearing. 'Please, Dai.' His little nose turned in disapproval. 'We are not children anymore.'

A handsome actor, who had played an implausibly conceited villain, jaunted among the crowd with a large floppy hat for donations. A swell of villagers gave appreciatively inasmuch as they were able. Approaching the Vornir siblings, the actor gave a little bow.

'How did you find our performance?' he asked them.

Daimonia noticed that among the jangling coins were donations of flowers and a potato. 'It pleased me very much,' she answered, squeezing her brother's arm. 'But wasn't it torture to play such a vile character?'

'I expect he enjoyed it,' Niklos mused. With a heartsick expression he tossed a silver denarius into the actor's hat.

'I don't choose my roles,' the actor admitted. 'But in the space between script and performance I may improvise just a little.'

Vornir Manor sat on a hill above the village, a stone haunt wrapped in vines and shadow. It had once been a watchtower from which a signal fire could alert the garrison of invasion. Now only ravens dutifully surveyed the coastal hills and forests. The dilapidated turrets remained a crumbling reminder of wars long past before the watchtower became the home of Jaromir's most feared citizen.

Jhonan Vornir was asleep when his grandchildren entered the draughty long-hall, his deep breaths whistling through broken teeth. The old man was slouched in his gnarled chair, his unkempt beard filthy with drunken vomit. Even in sleep Jhonan's silver-ringed hands were clenched around a mead horn and his prized Visoth war dagger. Several of his fingers were little more than stumps.

'I could kill him right now,' Niklos observed drily. 'Slit his throat while he sleeps.'

Daimonia raised her eyebrows at her brother's ridiculous posture. Niklos' chest and arms were puffed out like a threatened animal, his fingers twitching anxiously around the hilt of his sword. His teeth were bared like a wolf, but his innocent eyes were wide with fright.

'Then do it,' she challenged, her lip turning in mockery.

'I could.'

'Is this why you have come home? To kill an old man in his sleep?'

'No.' Niklos relaxed his shoulders and arms. 'I will be the better man.' He looked down his delicate nose if he were showing a great mercy.

Daimonia laughed scornfully. 'Have there ever been two people less willing to forgive each other?'

'You and mother?' Niklos suggested quickly. His cheeks immediately reddened with the ugliness of the remark.

Daimonia smiled, but her eyes were like prickly nettles. They had hurt each other before as only loved ones can: spoke cruelties instead of kindnesses and practised every snub and insult a brother and sister might share.

The fire crackled and popped, the familiar sound filling the silence between them. 'Come, brother,' she finally replied. 'Let us pretend we are children again.'

They sat together speaking softly, as was their habit when near the sleeping killer. They told each other lies about their mother and how she would soon return to love them as she had never done. It was a well-rehearsed exchange and comforting for all its deceit. Together again their faces glowed with youthful beauty, but the firelight revealed troubled wrinkles on Niklos' brow.

'You seem sad,' Daimonia observed. 'You have said nothing of your new life at Leechfinger or the honours and graces bestowed upon you as a Knight of the Accord.'

Niklos managed a lifeless smile. 'All arrogance,' he replied curtly.

'If you were the Prince of Dalibor, you would find a reason to be glum about it.' Daimonia laughed quietly. Her eyes went to their grandfather for a moment. Jhonan was still unconscious with drink, his bitter temper submerged in dreams of old wars. She prayed he would remain asleep until Niklos had left in the morning.

'I don't believe,' Niklos confided suddenly. His face was abashed and urgent. He was leaning close to her, as if for a kiss. 'I don't believe anymore.'

'Don't believe in what?'

'In the Accord,' Niklos confessed. His fingers went nervously to his cheek.

'What are you saying?' Daimonia was confused. The Accord was the foundation of society, the principles all citizens lived by. The Vornir family had fought for the Accord's establishment and defended it still.

'The Accord is a lie!' Niklos spat his treasonous words into the fire. 'It was designed to exploit men while using the language of serving them.'

Daimonia felt her hands tremble. Her beloved brother could be executed for such declarations. She stood and moved away, sensing a betrayal she could not yet fully fathom. She could hear the chorus of the old hymn in her mind; they had sung it a thousand times.

Whether given me by the Accord
The farmer's plough or soldier's sword,
Ever may my soul resign
Never questioning the great design.

'You speak against everything we have been taught,' Daimonia whispered. Even in her emerging anger, she was still mindful of how much worse this would be if Jhonan awakened. 'Do you think our mother fights for a lie?'

'Becoming a knight has allowed me to witness how the baron and his cronies really live.' Niklos made an ugly face. 'How they despise the poor and use the Accord to serve themselves and make orphans and widows of the rest! And as for the fate of those orphans...' Niklos' voice failed. His agitated fingers danced as if ready to pluck out his own eyes. 'I have such terrible suspicions that I cannot give them voice.'

'Where has all this come from, Niklos? These words are not your own thoughts. Who has confused you with all this doubt?'

'There are others, like-minded, who have helped me—'

'Fool,' she accused, rising with a dreadful expression of condemnation. 'Fool misguided by fools!'

'But that's just it, Dai. Don't you see? It is you who are fooled.'

Daimonia wished she were stronger, but her emotions swelled like vast tides, engulfing rationality. It was unthinkable that Niklos should be so frivolous with his life.

Without words for her feelings, she took flight from the manor and set out into the undiscovered night.

A drowsy mist had idled in from the coast, cooling the evening. The wispy air was illuminated by a brilliance of stars blooming in vast constellations. Daimonia knew that each star was a soul nestled in the cloak of the Goddess. One day she would join them or would witness their fall and the return of all things to chaos.

Brandishing a look of scorching intensity, Daimonia swept through the village, her hands cradled protectively around her heart. The girl wandered amid Jaromir's sleepy cottages, her fears mixed with stories of camaraderie and magic. Tonight the familiar met with an uncanny sense of unrealised potential. Some elusive treasure might be found or lost forever.

The actors had set tents atop the hill, a court of wind-rippled fabrics in lively theatrical colours. Daimonia climbed towards them, her long skirt clenched in her fists and her hair floating in the rising gale. In the impulsive fervour of the moment, she wanted to join the performers and play a role in their grand story. If her brother was to die a traitor's death, then Daimonia would prefer to live another life, to be someone else.

Daimonia reached the summit, her face wet with tears she could not recall crying. She felt not sad but empty and as dry as an unfilled cup.

The flapping fabrics revealed a single welcoming light. Within a womb-warm tent knelt a magnificent woman tying her hair elegantly into a plait. She was tall and powerful, perfect in form and beauty. Her gestures were full of grace and strength and Daimonia knew at once that this was the wonderful actress who had portrayed both the heroine and Goddess.

Daimonia watched with a kind of love. With all her heart she wanted to be this woman and everything she seemed to embody. In those sacred moments Daimonia imagined the powerful woman to be a self-created being – a player of roles, the ruler of her own thoughts and emotions, the creator of her own identity.

'Who's there?' a voice called out. The woman had seen her and was emerging from the tent, wrapped in a sovereign's cloak of silver and red. She seemed even taller now and her majestic brow lowered to focus upon Daimonia's blushing face.

'Dai Vornir.' Daimonia curtsied, remembering her manners. 'I've come to join the acting company.'

The woman laughed, fists on hips like a warrior. Her cheekbones were the most chiselled Daimonia had ever seen and gave mirth to all her expressions. 'Why would you want to do that?'

'I want to be part of your great story.'

The actress grinned as if colluding with an unspoken secret. Daimonia wondered what her history was, this glorious woman who could have become anybody.

'Why not let your life be the greatest story?' the actress suggested benignly. She lifted Daimonia's chin gently and then placed a single tender kiss on the girl's forehead.

Daimonia swelled inside at the generous affection. So perfect was the kindness that all troubles were scorched from her heart. A sigh loosed from her lips as she relished the lingering touch and affirmation, as if she were a baby floating amid the stars.

Then the wonderful moment was ruined, destroyed by the ominous noise of thundering hooves. Daimonia knew before looking that Niklos was the furious rider tearing through the village below, riding as if his resolve could rend the world in two. Niklos the traitor riding away forever.

An unkindness of manor ravens chased the boy's rippling cloak. The bloodthirsty warbirds were an omen of acrimony and violence. When travelling as three, as they flew tonight, it was a sign the War Goddess might awaken.

Boy, horse and birds were swallowed into the darkness. A winking star marked their passing as silence made an empty pit of the night.

Daimonia was alone, tottering precariously on the cusp of the hill. She stood imagining the whole world dead: homes empty, towns abandoned and the vast forests soundless. Black clouds dimmed the hilltop as she fled the scene.

She returned to Vornir Manor, trembling and cold, feeling afraid of the dark and of her creaky old room. The Eye of Ceresoph shone through the unshuttered window, illuminating the matriarchal image of her mother's face carved in immutable stone atop the bookshelf. She ran to the bust, running her fingers across Captain Catherine Vornir's imperious expression. Intimate with the stone, she traced the features reverently. Somewhere many miles away, was mother thinking of her too?

'Great mother,' Daimonia prayed, 'remember my foolish brother who has lost his way and protect us all from the deceptions of the wicked.'

The Murmurers

In the dripping dark, Daimonia sank from one dream to another, a midnight storm stirring her fears into nightmares. At the peak of each terror she woke like a drowning sailor, only to be dragged back under again.

Daimonia saw herself fight through a dense and sinuous forest. Beneath arched boughs she crawled and clambered, struggling amid thistles and thorns. Her knees and palms bled sorely as she wrestled with the strangulating terrain, desperation forcing her onwards. The forest was alive with atrocity, excruciating cries and glimpses of violence. She saw dismembered bodies nailed to a tree and witnessed a figure lashed furiously amid a mocking crowd. Each scene was a thorn spurring her towards some terrible vindication. Finally she found the deepest pit of the woods, wherein lay a smouldering sword half buried in the earth. Pleading voices begged Daimonia to seize the hissing blade and set loose, but when she drew it, the forest was flooded with rivers of blood.

A shock of lightning caught the girl clutching her blanket with panicked eyes. The grumbling thunder that followed was bellicose like an old man's ire. Daimonia's bedroom had been invaded by unfamiliar shadows and she closed her eyes rather than face them.

As the dreams swept her back down, Daimonia became aware of

something lurking beyond. A low murmur permeated each nightmare, the drone of things conspiring in the dark. Their plotting voices disturbed her, not with their malevolent tones, but through their indifference to the girl's existence. She had slipped behind the backdrop of life, to eavesdrop on the dead.

The storm subsided into a miserably dull morning and Daimonia returned to life with an exhausted sigh. Her eyes were puffy as she sniffed the moist morning air, her skin creased with the shapes of awkward sleep.

Invading rainwater streamed down the old stone walls and a troublesome leak splashed tears upon her mother's statue. A single raven lurked at her window, its black feathers glistening in the damp air.

Niklos is a traitor. The memory found Daimonia like an arrow and with it the conviction that her brother would be put to death. The fleeting joy of yesterday's festivities had drained away, like rain through the manor's archaic gutters.

Daimonia was tired, weary of her own weakness. She imagined there was an unsheathed sword within her heart, but she could not reach and draw it. Instead she seethed and ripped her dress, tearing it from her body, just as she might cast herself aside. 'I hate you,' she told the world.

She arose with stiff, frosty movements as if climbing from a crypt. Pale and trembling, the girl dressed in a simple robe and tried to tame her hair. It was a smoky tangled mess, defying the efforts of her fingers and comb.

Daimonia slipped from her room and descended through the draughty tower, her long legs picking a path down the uncertain steps.

She drifted into the hall, where her grandfather still slouched and slumbered.

'Grandfather, wake up!'

The old man revived slowly, advancing from blinks to twitches, gradually gathering the momentum to awake. Daimonia watched him patiently. She knew better than to disturb the old warrior before he recovered a sense of when and where he was.

Jhonan nodded an acknowledgement once his eyes found her. His stare then went to the shadows, seeking hidden threats in the dark.

Daimonia moved closer. Ignoring the searing stench of liquor, she hugged him, intimate with his rugged skin and wiry beard.

He held her briefly. 'What is it, Dai?'

'Nik was here.'

'Was?' He released her, hefting himself from the chair.

'You were asleep.' Her voice wavered between accusation and retreat.

Jhonan's face became a frightening thing met on a battlefield. He looked around for an enemy to destroy.

'Grandfather, I'm so worried,' Daimonia interceded, letting her lips tremble weakly. 'I think he's being led astray by some revolutionaries.'

A roar of laughter burst from the old warrior. 'Gentle Niklos a revolutionary?' The derisive guffaw echoed coldly through the hall. 'Our helpless Nik, a Vendicatori conspirator? If he had the courage for it, that would at least be something.'

'Grandfather, I'm serious!' Daimonia felt her cheeks redden. 'He'll get himself killed!'

'Silly girl!' Jhonan waved the idea away. 'Don't you see this is exactly

14

what Niklos wants? He hopes to hurt me with this foolish lie.'

'No, this isn't about you!'

'Isn't it?' Jhonan toyed with the silver beads in his beard. 'He's been a guest in my home without a single word to me. He has put the fear of Baoth into you and now threatens to disgrace the Vornir name? The boy will do anything to rouse sympathy and attention.'

'Why would he want your attention?' Daimonia bared her teeth. 'Does he hope for another beating?'

'Boys need to be hardened else the world eat them!' Jhonan defended. 'That's how my father was and it did me no harm!'

Daimonia said nothing until they had both cooled. Once any Vornir's shield was up, there was little space for reasoning. When Jhonan had unclenched his fists, she chose her moment. 'Niklos claims the Baron of Leechfinger is corrupt.'

Jhonan turned his face and strode towards the fireplace. Once a powerful knight, his muscles and tendons now bore the penalty of age. With slow strength he leaned against the wall, glaring at the embers with a distant eye.

'I met Volk Leechfinger once. I didn't like him.'

'Why would Niklos be afraid for the orphans?' Daimonia persisted.

'The baron is capable of any atrocity. I'll concede that.'

'We're going,' Daimonia decided. 'We're going to Leechfinger today.'

'Leechfinger is no place for you. If Niklos must be found, I'll be the one to go.'

'Is the world beyond Jaromir really so terrible?'

'Yes, but that's not the issue here. This'll go better if I'm not worrying about you as well.'

'Is that all there is for me? To be a weak and sheltered thing, hiding here, afraid to live?'

'No, Daimonia.'

'Then let me help my brother. I too am a Vornir!'

Jhonan's horse was an ill-tempered mare. Despite much whistling and coaxing, they lost an hour chasing her around the field. Eventually they got the creature bridled and ready to lead their old wagon.

As they trundled through the village, they saw the travelling players packing up to leave. The fancifully dressed performers sang as they worked, reprising a song from the beginning of the heroine's journey. Daimonia stared at the exotic characters longingly; theirs was the life she wanted for herself, a colourful adventure with interesting companions. Why did she have this terrible heartache instead?

Her eyes sought the powerful actress and found the woman lifting and labouring, easily keeping pace with the strongest men. Daimonia wondered whether to call out but felt afraid of somehow diminishing the perfect moment they had shared. After a brief indecision, she started waving, increasing her enthusiasm anxiously when the actress did not notice. A familiar and lonely ache teased her heart. Daimonia wished she could see her own face and know whether she was lovable.

'Stop that,' Jhonan said, lowering her hand.

'But, Grandfather, you didn't see the performance! You don't know the wonderful story.'

'I know the myths.' Jhonan licked at the spaces between his sparse teeth. 'You'll have story enough to tell when I get hold of your foolish brother!'

Daimonia noticed two armoured knights helping the actors to prepare for departure. They were young and clean-shaven, smiling and joking as they disassembled the fabulous tents.

'Way Knights,' Jhonan sneered. 'Looks like the players intend to tour the coast.' He spat abruptly. 'What fools! Who would attempt that journey for the sake of a story?'

'Shouldn't we employ Way Knights too?'

'Chrestos' beard!' He raised a black eyebrow. 'What kind of man would I be if I couldn't get my own granddaughter to Leechfinger? Now take the reins while I have a drink.'

That night they hunted game together, prowling through the bountiful wood. In a star-bright clearing a single deer stood breathing the invigorating air.

'So beautiful and proud,' Daimonia whispered, her hands trembling on her bow.

'Take the shot.'

'A stag is a feast for ten people,' said Daimonia. 'Not two.'

'The Goddess is generous.'

They ate at first in silence, Daimonia's imagination returning constantly to her fear. What would become of Niklos? A repetitious cycle of prayers rolled around her mind, imploring the Goddess to show her the way.

'You were a child when you last left Jaromir,' Jhonan recalled. 'You probably don't even remember.'

'Of course I remember.' Daimonia's face became childlike. 'We went to Littlecrook for a fair. Niklos and I cried when it was time to leave, and Mother became so angry that she ripped out chunks of her own hair, shrieking at us.'

Jhonan said nothing. The night fell from cold to cuttingly chill.

'We must bring Niklos back home,' Daimonia declared after a long think. 'Keep him out of trouble. He was never cut out to be a knight. In fact, he would never have even left if it wasn't for—'

'He can't come home,' Jhonan interrupted.

'Can't?' Daimonia recoiled as if slapped.

'He can't come home. He is sworn to the Accord and he must serve where and when instructed. Just like your mother.'

'Then what do you intend to do?'

'Kill him, of course.'

'I don't like it when you talk that way.'

'You think I should let him destroy my name? Destroy your mother's reputation?'

'You wouldn't kill your own grandson.'

Jhonan tilted his head, appearing to turn the suggestion over in his mind. He held his hands before the campfire as shadows rippled across his body.

'There's a thing that lives in some men.' Jhonan stared through the fire, his mouth turned in disgust. 'It covers itself in flesh so as to pass for human, but it is not. It can feign our emotions, but it does not feel them.

18

Instead it stares out through our eyes with a greed that is never satisfied. And if someone frustrates that greed? Then the terrible thing will show itself.'

'I don't understand,' Daimonia admitted.

'Know this,' Jhonan told her. 'If Niklos provokes the baron, the consequences will find us all.'

The Cage

The bridge to Leechfinger was a clogged artery, clotted with people, horses, cows and pigs. Running from Littlecrook village, it struck across the great river and into the tiered city whose turrets poked rudely at the heavens.

Daimonia and Jhonan left their horse and wagon with the Blightwaters of Littlecrook and joined the funnel of shuffling travellers. Here traffic from all the southern villages fought to get either in or out of the city. As the Vornirs tried to advance among the shoving crowd, Daimonia found herself in close proximity with scores of strangers, becoming intimate with their elbows and breath without the exchange of a single pleasantry.

'Stay close,' Jhonan instructed as they bore forwards. 'And keep your purse closer.'

Traders had established an inconvenient cluster of stalls all along the parapet, leaving barely a wagon's width for traffic. Nobles and peasants jostled on the slimy thoroughfare. Horses defecated. The reeking stench of sweat and dung permeated everything, exacerbated by the brown river churning beneath.

Stuck in the tide of bodies, Daimonia tried to squeeze her way forwards. How different this was from the wide-open spaces of Jaromir, where it was rarely necessary to come within two paces of another person. She wanted to weep with frustration but noticed that Jhonan seemed faintly amused by the arduous task. The old man's eyes glistened as he used his shoulder to force a path steadily onward. He clutched Daimonia's wrist in one hand and pulled her along in his wake.

Daimonia felt her cheeks redden and surrendered any sense of autonomy to her grandfather. He was strong and decisive in this place, where she felt wrong-footed and weak. She allowed him to drag her up through the mob, captive to his determination.

'So many people,' Daimonia worried. 'How will we ever find Nik?'

'We'll try the Garden of Shame.'

Daimonia scowled. 'That doesn't sound like somewhere we'd find my brother!'

Jhonan nodded grimly; he drew the girl close. They might have been in their own world. 'There's an inevitability about some men. They set their sights on self-destruction, but when she shows her face, they greet her with surprise!'

'You can't be talking about our Nik.' Daimonia pulled her wrist free from the old man's fist.

'Wait and see.'

Their progress along the bridge slowed when they fell behind a strapping Visoth, whose straw-coloured hair draped over a cloak of tanned skin. The foreigner used his size and broad shoulders to block the Vornirs whenever they tried to pass.

'We won't make the city before nightfall,' Jhonan grumbled. 'Not stuck behind this slow ox!'

'Perhaps Nik is at the barracks. I assume the Knights of the Accord own property here?'

'Property? Hah!' Jhonan blew snot from one nostril. 'You're not wrong about that!' He tried to advance but again was blocked by the hulking figure.

'Stop kicking!' the Visoth turned around to holler in Jhonan's face. His accent was strange to Daimonia's ear, each word so heavy it could have been the end of a sentence. 'Be patient, old man, or I'll ride you up and down this bridge!' The Visoth stooped towards Jhonan until their foreheads were touching. His eyes were an ardent green and would have been alluring on a face not twisted with anger.

Jhonan yanked the outlander's beard, yielding an expression of anguish from the throbbing face. He tugged hard, swinging the man into a stall crowded with hanging meat. Flesh, canopy and customers collapsed, haunches of beef plopping into the river below.

'Bloody migrants!' Jhonan fought through the crowd with renewed vigour.

Finally they reached the gate, where armoured militants swaggered and drank, demanding a toll for every creature entering. A green flag above the gatehouse depicted the Leechfinger heraldry – a severed hand with one finger pointing skyward.

'What's your business in Leechfinger?' the militant captain asked Jhonan.

'I'm here to kill my grandson.'

The captain snorted and waved them both through.

They emerged from the shadow of the portcullis to witness a slow struggle between construction and nature. Great paving slabs lay across the length and breadth of the plaza but had been thrown into disarray by the intrusion of thick implacable roots. The result was a hazardously uneven walkway around which buildings sat crookedly and visitors stumbled.

A gang of beggars, some twenty or thirty strong, worked these city outskirts. They dressed in hooded cloaks covered with dozens of haphazard pockets.

'Why would you say that?' Daimonia challenged as they entered the busy plaza.

'Say what?'

'This talk of killing Niklos.' Daimonia glared at the old man. 'I don't find it funny.'

'I already told you. If Nik is pronounced a traitor, the whole village will be punished. I can't allow that to happen.'

'Scuse me,' a coarse voice intruded. 'D'ya have jus' a few coins to spare, miss?' The beggar's eyes were all over Daimonia as he approached with cupped hands. He took inventory of the eye-shaped brooch on her cloak and the buttons on her dress.

Daimonia reached for her purse, but Jhonan intervened, shoving the hooded figure back. The beggar tripped on the paving, landing on the back of his shoulders as his legs kicked the sky. Stolen treasures spilled from his many pockets.

'I'll cut ya!' the beggar howled. 'Cut ya, dirty bastard!'

'Why did you do that?' Daimonia rounded on her grandfather.

'Keep moving,' Jhonan urged as others began to take notice. They turned into a crooked street, avoiding pits, pickpockets and brazen rats. The old man tried to take Daimonia's hand, but she turned away, folding her arms across her chest.

'I tried to guide your brother,' Jhonan complained. 'Tried to avoid a day like this one.'

'Yes, it takes a great warrior to beat a child.'

'Not this again!' Jhonan threw up his arms in protest.

'The person with the most power is always right. Is that what you wanted Nik to believe?'

'You're shoving words into my mouth.'

A unit of Knights of the Accord marched past, intent on some decisive purpose. They wore tailed iron hats, chain armour and white heraldic tabards. Pounding through the street, they battered anyone too slow to move aside. Daimonia stared at each shadowed face, hoping to see her brother among them. She found only the hard stares of strangers.

'Is there some relationship between might and virtue?' Daimonia wondered aloud.

'These questions of yours.' Jhonan began to shake with irritation.

24

'They don't connect to the world I know. They're not useful in the panic of battle or when you're wearing the remains of your comrades.' His lips frothed with bubbles of spittle. 'They belong to a world of ideas, not the true world of mud, blood and men.'

Maybe this will connect, Daimonia seethed inwardly. *Hurt my brother and I hurt you. Can you understand that? Does that ring true for you?* But she had the sense not to say it.

A towering wall divided the city, a second gate defending the higher tier. Huge bald faces were engraved in the stone, their mouths open to vomit streams of refuse upon the streets below. The waste collected in open gutters, bulging right before the Vornirs' feet as they approached.

'I can't stand it,' Daimonia gasped, pinching her nose. The obscene smell, evident since their arrival, had become overwhelmingly nauseating. She pinched her nose and stuck out her tongue at the dire stench. 'I won't stay a single night in this place.'

'Find strength,' Jhonan demanded.

They negotiated their way through the inner gate with a show of Jhonan's knightly insignia and some denarii.

'Don't forget to wash your hands,' a militant told them as he jingled the small bribe. He tipped his head towards a large stone hand-bath, the sides of which resembled giant petals.

Daimonia stared into the dirty water – a broth of mud, blood and saliva. Odd shapes floated in the grisly stew. The militants were watching her, frowning against the sunlight as they stared. She dipped her fingers into the warm liquid fleetingly before shaking them dry. She

25

felt polluted by the little ritual, poisoned by the taint of other people's filth.

Jhonan strolled past, contributing only a pearl of phlegm to the pool.

A great stairway rose from the lower districts, ascending towards magnificent columns framed by sky. Jhonan found a different curse for every single step of their ascent and the Vornirs were both heaving with sweat before they reached the top. Their ordeal was rewarded by cool, clear air and a panoramic view of the contorted streets below. From here the lower city appeared a grey and grotesque maze in which thousands of tiny people were trapped. Daimonia wanted to break down the walls and let them all escape.

'Don't let yourself get carried away,' Jhonan cautioned. 'If Nik is here, I mean.'

Daimonia turned to regard the high gardens of Leechfinger. Here the elegant homes of the city aldermen were wreathed in rippling foliage. Nobles toured the grounds, fat with health and attended by trains of servants.

'Over there.' Jhonan pointed. 'In the shadow of the hero-temple.'

Divine Chrestos stood enormous in white stone, presiding over the gardens. One hand was at his chin while another was tipped towards his tiny genitals. Daimonia craned her neck to look at the godly statue. To the girl his wide-open smile seemed unashamedly lecherous, unrestrained in its ebullient lust. Beyond his towering form the clouds looked like waves viewed from beneath the ocean.

At the statue's base a maxim was inscribed in stone. In carefully chiselled letters it read WHO IS CHRESTOS?

'What does it mean?' Daimonia asked as they approached. 'The inscription.'

'Eh? It's some kind of challenge to men. I don't know. Do I look like a philosopher?'

'I'm not sure what that is.'

'Someone worried about truth,' Jhonan replied with annoyance in his voice. 'Questioning every little thing all the time.'

Beneath the statue they came upon a well-protected garden patrolled by militants and knights alike. Daimonia counted ten fighters standing sentry; some of them were veterans missing a hand or eye.

The garden was adorned with living ornaments. Men were entrapped in thin cages, so restrictive that only standing was possible. Some prisoners had discovered ways to relax into this confinement, adopting strange postures to relieve their own weight. Others clung to their bars with livid intensity, spitting obscenities at all who met their stare.

Splendidly attired nobles wandered around the captured men, frittering away the afternoon with chatter. Occasionally they would stop to comment on an especially notorious or interesting prisoner before resuming their own concerns.

A solitary knight stood, confined but upright, in his own cage. The crude incarceration had not tempered his pride. As nobles approached, he returned their stares with a look of searing scrutiny, as if they were grotesque oddities within his court. Young masters and their ladies turned away in disquiet, somehow shamed by the unbroken youth.

'Nik!' Daimonia called, rushing to her brother. 'Niklos!'

The startled knight turned to his sister, his expression losing all restraint. 'Oh, Daimonia! Why have you come here?' Niklos tried in vain to squeeze himself through the cage. 'It breaks my heart to see you.' His voice was musical with feeling.

Daimonia touched his face tenderly through the bars. 'Don't be sad,' she consoled. 'We're here to rescue you.'

'Rescue?' Jhonan interrupted. He made the sign of silence with his finger.

Niklos' expression tightened. 'Why are you here, old man?'

'Why?' Jhonan looked uneasily at the surrounding guards before meeting Niklos' stare. Already they were attracting looks of suspicion. 'I'm here because your sister demanded it. But mostly to see for myself what you have become.'

'Then enjoy it!' Niklos challenged. 'You told me I was nothing. Those were your exact words. And here I am. Nothing. Just as you expected.'

Jhonan leaned away, blinking. There was the merest glimmer of pain before he retorted, 'The Niklos I knew was a weak boy, masking fear with arrogance. Is that boy here now?'

'Come closer and find out!'

'Enough!' Daimonia stepped between them. 'I've had a lifetime of your bickering! We are all of the same blood. Old Vornir blood, the descendants of wolves. People once feared our name, yet it seems our family has no other pursuit than to wound each other.'

'Perhaps I was born wounded.' Niklos continued to pity himself. 'Do you know why I'm here? They say I'm a murderer. And worse than that, a traitor.' Niklos wore a pained smile as he looked around the garden.

'And now I'm a curiosity for the amusement of these maggots.'

'You're no murderer!' Daimonia protested. 'You're the gentlest person I've ever known.'

'I'm guilty of both charges. I killed a Seidhr not a mile from where we are standing. Stabbed her to death in the streets.'

'But why, Nik?' Daimonia's dark scowl was not unlike Jhonan's. 'Why would you do such a thing?'

The clouds beyond the Chrestos statue were darkening, congealing into a beggar's cloak around the deity's throat.

'Stay awhile and I will share my confession.'

Confession

'Stealing children and fighting women were not what I anticipated as a boy dreaming of knighthood,' Niklos began bitterly. He strained against the bars as if memory might release him.

'Do you remember our mother's initiation as a Knight of the Accord?' he asked Daimonia. 'We were at the Exalt Temple in Kraljevic, a place I will never forget. I remember feeling awed by the authority of those colossal walls and towering steeples, fascinated by the great archways and tiny doors leading to mysterious places.'

'I remember too.' Daimonia laughed sadly. 'I can still picture the High Adjurator wreathed in gleaming treasure while the workers swept the floor around him!'

'Yes.' Niklos smiled. 'You and I sat beside a row of armoured knights and I was curiously admiring the rings of their armour. One of the knights saw me staring and loaned me his gauntlet to play with. I could put both my fists inside that metal glove!

'The ceremony began and all the new Accord Knights marched in proudly. There was our mother, Lady Catherine Vornir, joining hands with Prince Moranion! The music and ceremony were like a rousing hymn to my spirit. I was peeking into a more exciting life that I wanted to be part of. My heart felt such conviction that it might have been my own initiation.

'When my own day finally came, it surpassed my expectations. I remember donning this mail for the first time and relishing its assuring weight. I felt incredible, like an unkillable thing of bone and metal. The armour changed the way I stood, the way I walked and held myself. But even that was nothing to the experience of dressing in the tabard of the Accord. I had become part of a long line of champions, already sharing in their honour. And the sword—'

'What vanity!' Jhonan's laughter disturbed the whole garden. 'In all my years I have never heard such vain boasting!'

'You may call it that, but for me it was closer to innocence.' Niklos' unguarded expression retreated into a shielded frown.

'Confusing your garments for personal merit? That smells more like arrogance to me.'

'Grandfather, please,' Daimonia interceded. 'Let him speak.'

'Perhaps you never knew it, old man, as no one counts you as a friend. The feeling of camaraderie, leaving the barracks with those you have trained with. The surety of the horse; the shy smiles of pretty girls in the street.'

'I've raised a poet instead of a warrior.' Jhonan made the sign of a man pleasing himself.

Passing nobles tutted at Jhonan's uncouth behaviour, but Daimonia glimpsed panic hiding behind her grandfather's bluster. She had seen this vulnerability before, when her mother had left Jhonan to raise her children alone.

'My illusions were short lived,' Niklos conceded. 'I had hoped to join our mother in Khorgov but was posted here to Leechfinger. Not so very far from home and an unglamorous placement that had other knights scoffing at my misfortune.'

'You wanted to be far away?' Daimonia wondered.

'I wanted something equal to my own feeling. An opportunity that could live up to the passion I would bring to it.'

'And did you find it?'

'No. The Leechfinger Accord Knights immediately held me in contempt because of my inexperience and enthusiasm. They told me I was arrogant and lacked humility, whereas I found them idle and dull. They wouldn't do a single thing without being compelled. On my very first night they sent me out alone, to support the city militants on their evening patrol.'

'I wish I could have seen that!' Jhonan revelled. 'I bet the scrappers and drunkards of Leechfinger enjoyed our pretty Nik!'

'The militants found me amusing,' Niklos admitted. 'They were older men, whereas I was not much more than a shivering boy. They were also very drunk. Drunker even than those we would be confronting. They pulled at my hair and cheeks and made every attempt to undermine me.

'Our patrol began and the night poured out its armies of men made monstrous by drink. There were roaring disputes over street territories, savage fights and awful crimes. Our work was to defend the estates that had paid for our protection. We fell into an ambush of spitting, kicking fighters and spent the night brawling in the gutters. In the morning my armour was caked with shit and my face was black with swollen lumps. Even so I felt a strange exhilaration as I explored my missing teeth and bruises. It hurt like bloody Thalatte, but the city had initiated me in its own way.

'The very next night my fortune changed entirely, or so I thought. I was given the prestigious honour of accompanying Baron Leechfinger on his travels around the city. I joined a group of veteran knights who were the baron's personal guards. We waited for ages in a luxurious carpeted chamber for the baron to prepare, watching his children weave baskets for the cat-burning festival. The baron finally arrived, wearing the full regalia of his office, and greeted each knight very warmly as if we were all comrades and equals.

'Our journey was to a half-timbered house full of young maidens. I can still picture the tentative smiles on their scabby lips. As he had done with the knights, Baron Leechfinger greeted each of the girls and was especially charming and gracious. Afterwards he retired to a room with several of the young women in his company.

'I asked the other knights what was to be done now, a question that provoked great hilarity among them. As grunts and sighs filled the air, they covered their mouths with their hands, chuckling at my embarrassment.

'A procession of privileged nobles penetrated the scene. They arrived muttering to each other as they removed feathered hats and cloaks. They too were there to enjoy the girls forced by poverty.'

'What did you do?'

'I did nothing. I took my lead from the other knights and colluded with everything, one dismal day after another.'

'How miserable,' Daimonia commiserated. 'I would've wanted to burn the place down.'

'It's a frightening thing, Dai. What you will go along with if no one else speaks out. And things became much worse when I was assigned to support the Benevolent Sisters of the Seidhr Order. I arrived at the Seidhr Halls, already slightly less the man than I had been months before. These chambers were full of busy women, crying babies and raucous children. They had adapted the imagery of Great Mother Cerenox in their tapestries and sculpture. The symbol of a huge pair of hands cupping a tiny baby recurred, sometimes reinterpreted as a protective fist with the child within.

'The Seidhr workers were faceless, each hiding their beauty behind a reflective mask. Their robes were long and modest. Only their hair allowed for vanity, often tied in elaborate plaits and patterns.

'Here I was introduced to Sister Osmanna, a fervent Seidhr initiate whom I would be protecting as she went about her duties. When we met, she was shepherding a class of young girls through the chambers. These had been given to the Seidhr to train in their arts, fresh acolytes for the Leechfinger coven. Osmanna's very first words to me were "I hate children!" She then began to explain all the duties of a Knight of the Accord, as if I were in need of her instruction!

'Sister Osmanna described her own responsibilities as finding lost children and placing them in good homes. Wherever there were orphans, the Seidhr Order would intervene. I became part of a group of six knights escorting Osmanna as she carried out her duties in the shires. Even the most senior among us was subordinate to the Seidhr worker. We patrolled with a convoy of caged carriages. It was explained to me that distressed children would sometimes need to be contained and that this was for their own safety.

'At first it seemed I had found my place. We rescued two young brothers who had been hiding since the Baoth raided their village. These boys had survived by their own cunning for weeks. They were thrilled to be travelling with knights and even bore the cages gleefully. We scared off youths who were dropping rocks on travellers. We helped a family who had lost everything to fire.

'But something went horribly wrong. After a few weeks we had not gathered many orphans and Osmanna made the decision to remove children from their families. I know that's not unheard of in some situations, but for the life of us we couldn't understand the choices being made. Imagine having to fight off honest farmers as we stole away their daughters! And not just the men but literally brawling with anguished mothers as we seized their children!

'There were fierce arguments and many hard words spoken among us. Sister Osmanna claimed she had the art of seeing what men hid in their hearts. She claimed she was rescuing these children and that anyone saying otherwise was a traitor.

'We arrived at Leechfinger like a gang of returning kidnappers, with the captured children kicking and screaming within the wagon cells. We had not placed a single child in a new home. You should have heard their cries and seen their miserable faces coming into this disgusting place, torn away from their loving mothers.

'Before we could even reach the Seidhr Halls, we were surrounded by men from the crassest noble houses: lavishly dressed Guldslags, greedy

Likoths and fat Averites. They were vetting the prettiest children, examining teeth and hands, and remarking on who was most pleasing. Worst of all there was talk of an auction.

'Not a single word passed between us knights as we drove the wagons through the back streets. Each man drew his dagger and plunged it into the Seidhr. I have never heard such screams or seen such determination to survive, but we stuck her till she was dead.'

'You might have raised a grievance, as was your right,' Jhonan grumbled.

'A grievance?' Niklos was exasperated, clenching the bars with trembling fists. 'Have you listened to one word, old man? The Accord equates virtue with rank. Only a fool would pit lowly knights against Seidhr workers and lords in a court!'

'Look what you've accomplished.' Jhonan gestured to the cages. 'You've killed yourself! You've shamed your name!' He leaned menacingly close. '*My* name has been shamed!'

'Enjoy it,' Niklos snapped back. 'You said I'd come to nothing and you were right!'

'But what happened to the children?' Daimonia demanded.

'We separated and returned the children to their homes. I just had escorted a sweet girl back to her family when I came to find you in Jaromir. I thought that would be the last time I ever looked upon your face. The baron's men caught up with me that same evening.'

Daimonia felt as if she would burst. 'What you did was courageous!' She shot a disdainful glance at Jhonan. 'They acted out of expediency, for the children!'

'Perhaps so, but the Accord will now be obeyed.' Jhonan pulled at his beard-rings. 'Nik has two choices: either trial by combat against an Executioner Knight or else a trial of words and the judgement of the Lawspeaker.'

'Can't you fight for him, Grandfather?'

'A knight must stand for himself.' Jhonan shook his head. 'But this boy has no chance against the Executioners. They are gladiators who excel at slaughtering other knights. Niklos would make a fine plaything for any one of them.'

'And yet I have decided to fight,' Niklos revealed.

'Don't be foolish.' Jhonan lowered his voice. 'You were both tutored, taught to read and write, to learn the Accord and the histories. Your mother insisted on that at least.' He leaned close to the bars, spitting instruction through his beard. 'Your arena is reason and argument, not axes and swords. Chrestos curse me for not admitting it sooner. You must take the trial of words.'

'If I die, then I die,' Niklos declared. 'But a Lawspeaker has the power to damn me to Archonia. Only a fool would gamble with that prospect! No, freedom must be won by the sword.'

The Meat Pit

'The Meat Pit,' Jhonan snarled. 'This is no place for a Vornir to die.'

They stood by the arena's edge, Daimonia squashed against her grandfather's chest as he put his arms about her protectively. They were swamped by a mob of excited peasants, all desperate to get the best view of the forthcoming bloodshed. Those able to get closest hung tightly to the inner wall, unwilling to be pried off lest they surrender their advantageous view.

The Meat Pit was an oval amphitheatre filled with sand, small rocks and fragments of bone. From opposite sides portcullis gates stood ready to admit the condemned. Tusks protruded along the filthy walls, cruelly placed to threaten throats and buttocks. Ascending tiers of seating rose gradually to the royal circle reserved for the highest nobility.

Enormous animal-skin drums were situated above either end of the pit. Burly Afreyan musicians struck the drums with giant sticks, producing a rhythm that matched Daimonia's galloping heart. Visoth long-horns, tall as horses, blew deep notes from their serpentine lungs. The music was bold and primal like the war song of a vengeful warrior. Children laughed, women shrieked and men thumped each other and even themselves. The cumulative impression was of impending catastrophic doom.

The malevolent anthem climaxed in the arrival of a tall figure standing in the highest tier and making the sign of the victor with his thumb and fist. Like everyone, Daimonia found herself drawn to the sight, scrutinising the man she had already decided to loathe. Baron Volk Leechfinger had the body of a once mighty warrior, long since enlarged by food and wine. There was so much of him that his embroidered toga could have clothed two or three lesser men. His scalp and beard were completely shaved, accentuating the prettiness of his eyes, which were painted black and crowned with long curling lashes. His style and proportions gave him grandeur, but his face was too animated to ever be considered wholesome. Not a moment passed without his lewd expression evolving into even more carnal and suggestive forms.

The baron waved to the baying crowd, surveying their excitement and meeting it with a rapacious smile. Seeming to orchestrate their cheers, he hooked the attention of the entire gathering and ultimately their silence. Thus gratified, he sat himself in the luxurious royal box, surrounded by an entourage of politicians and other creatures.

The ceremony began with a stoning. Baskets of rocks were distributed among the citizens by sweating slaves. Families scrambled to grab fistfuls of the sharpest and heaviest stones. A portcullis grated open and a group of prisoners were spurred into the arena by the spears of the militants. The competition began immediately, with the audience launching rocks energetically at the terrified targets. The prisoners wept and ran, shielding their heads with their arms as stones rained down from all sides of the pit.

Daimonia was aghast at the brutality. She watched the fervour of the crowd, finding it vulgar and repulsive. She witnessed their strained, almost sensual faces, their tongues extended, eyes hot with desire. Many were in states of undress, some even caressing themselves as the rocks shattered bones and smashed faces.

'Crooks, anarchists and molesters of various kinds,' Jhonan commented. 'All fit for death.'

Daimonia was unsure of whom Jhonan was speaking. 'I cannot watch,' she croaked, hiding her face in her hands. Tender tears wet her fingers.

Jhonan tossed a glazed look at the crowd. 'All life is violent,' he remarked bluntly. 'This is the closest some'll get to smashing their own fears in the face.'

A great cheer rolled around the arena. Afraid to look, Daimonia squeezed her eyes tightly shut.

'Cracked that one's head like clay!' Jhonan seemed impressed. The image was offered like a curse to Daimonia, who was forced to imagine it.

'I cannot stay.' Daimonia wept. She pushed against the human wall but was unable to breach the crowd.

'Wait!' Jhonan urged. 'Niklos arrives!'

A sloping figure emerged from behind a portcullis to be met with a vociferous barrage of jeering and booing. He peered up at the yelling hundreds who had come to watch him die, a thin veneer of bravery on his face. The militants had mockingly dressed him in a tabard of the Knights Anarchist, a parody of the heraldry of a true knight. His armour had been removed, but he had been provided a broadsword and shield, his only allies in the trial ahead.

'Nik!' Daimonia cried, but her voice was lost in the cacophony.

Some who still had rocks threw them into the arena, though that stopped when Baron Leechfinger arose. The baron fixed his impassioned gaze upon the youth. 'No betrayer is worse than those we have held to our bosom,' he began, raising one fist to his chest. 'Young Vornir was afforded every advantage, coming from a reputable family and having been granted the prestigious rank of Knight of the Accord. But just as cream will spoil, so a privileged youth may become corrupt.'

The crowd were listening like dogs to their master, allowing their hatred to be piqued so as to better enjoy the violence ahead. 'Vornir murdered remorselessly,' the baron continued, feeding their appetite for slander. 'He stole children from the care of the Seidhr. He corrupted other knights, some of whom have already met a tragic end in this very place.' The baron's voice became thick with emotion, as if he genuinely believed his own contrivance. 'But perhaps it is we who have failed young Vornir? Not done enough to lead him on the right path? Not loved enough? Not given enough?'

The mob became much agitated by this line of reasoning and cried out in wrath. They demanded Niklos' execution and not just his death, but his mutilation and crucifixion.

'I implore you now,' the baron addressed Niklos. 'Beg for the forgiveness of these good people and you will meet a clean death. Your body will be burned in honour of the Goddess and your family exonerated of any complicity.'

'I regret nothing!' Despite his defiance, Niklos sounded timid and wavering in the amphitheatre. 'The Accord is a lie!' He said the words, but his voice dwindled almost to silence. Nevertheless the young man summoned enough phlegm to spit upon the sand.

'Entreat our mercy,' the baron coaxed, as if to a stubborn child. 'If not for yourself, then for the sake of your family.'

Niklos' eyes found his sister. 'I will prove my innocence in combat!' he shouted. This time his voice rang clear and brave, but his legs were trembling visibly.

'So be it.' The baron made a show of surrendering to Niklos' wishes, washing his hands in an ornamental bowl. 'I call upon Prettanike to administer sentence.' He plucked a pear from a servant's dish and regained his seat, biting hungrily. Juice and drool washed down his chin.

From the pit's under-chambers came the grind of a winch turning. A second portcullis cranked open and a sepulchral stench exuded from the depths.

Knight Executioner Prettanike strode into the pit, the bones of dead warriors crunching beneath her calloused feet. She was tall and athletic with thick thighs and muscular calves. Armoured scales glistened along her left arm, leading to a shield-like pauldron that curved to guard her neck. Her leather gauntlets clenched a long partisan headed by a trinity of blades. Her head was protected by an elaborate helmet, from which her red hair plumed like a continuous spout of blood. Only her lips were visible beneath the ornate headpiece, pressed firm in resolution.

'They humiliate Nik by making him fight a woman,' Jhonan moaned resentfully.

'Look at her.' Daimonia shivered. 'As fierce as Cere-Thalatte!'

Prettanike's swaggering advance cast a shadow over the rock-ruined corpses that lay strewn around the sand. The crowd began to clap in time with her steps, as did the Afreyan musicians beating their oversized drums.

Niklos looked to the crowd and then to the gate. He began to step backwards, retreating while keeping his eyes locked to the Executioner's movement. She was approaching with a slow surety, inevitable as death. He fell back behind his shield, poised to thrust at his towering foe.

Prettanike charged, horse-like, across the sand. Muscles propelled her momentum. Drums crashed.

Niklos leaned into the shield, consolidating his body into a compact hammer of rage. The combatants collided, skin meeting skin, flesh rippling with the impact. A fist found Niklos' face, a knee his gut. He swung with his shield, but the gladiator was already a step away, her foot raised to stamp on his chest.

Ribs fractured. Niklos stumbled over a fresh corpse and in the confusion barely glimpsed the blade spearing towards his head. His face was lacerated, making a bloody mouth of his cheek.

Daimonia touched her own face in sympathy, her lips quivering with fright. 'Please live,' she implored. 'Fight and live!'

Niklos rolled and leaped away, jogging to the edge of the arena. He wiped his bleeding face with the back of his hand, blinking through the pain.

Prettanike held her ground, allowing the crowd time to mock Niklos' hasty retreat. She steered her long weapon towards the boy, as if keeping a lethargic animal at bay.

Niklos appeared to be thinking desperately, caught between retreat and battle. All the names of the Goddess rolled off his tongue imploringly.

'Come on!' Prettanike taunted. She stretched out her arms, seeming to invite attack.

Niklos rushed in with a sequence of thrusts and slashes that seemed rehearsed and unnatural. Prettanike turned his blade aside and thwacked his backside with the rear of her weapon. The crowd cheered.

Niklos fell back, his chest rising with heavy breaths while Prettanike resumed her slow advance.

Niklos was visibly tiring, his movements becoming slower and more burdensome. His sword dragged in the sand. His bloodstained mouth hung open, drawing huge breaths.

'Fight!' Jhonan bellowed, his cheeks flaming red. 'Go on, boy, fight!' The old man was striking at the air, as if it were his battle.

Desperation filled Niklos' eyes. Throwing all caution aside, he charged with an energetic overhead swipe. Prettanike raised her partisan, blocking the blow, and then struck with the triple-bladed end. The cut was not deep but severed the belt of Niklos' trousers and they began to sag awkwardly, slipping down his thighs. Enormous laughter erupted from the crowd as Niklos was forced to defend himself with one hand hoisting his trousers up. A Visoth horn-blower produced a mocking noise like passing wind. Men held their bellies and women threw back their hair as they taunted the inadequate fighter.

Daimonia's heart stung as she saw the despair on Niklos' face. This was to be his death and there was no nobility in it, only pain, humiliation and infamy. A lifetime of vulnerability was rushing up on her brother, culminating in one moment of absolute defeat.

Prettanike thrust her whole body into the strike. She drove the partisan deep into Niklos' stomach. A glimmer of satisfaction played on the Knight Executioner's lips as she twisted the weapon and wrenched it free of the dying youth, releasing a gush of blood and flapping entrails. Her blades now bore a bloody flag ripped from rent tabard.

The world inside Daimonia ended. Memories putrefied, decaying her will to live. With her last strength she drew herself up onto the wall and toppled into the pit. She surrendered to the bitter sun as she fell into the arena, ready to die alongside Niklos.

Scrambling amid the debris, she crawled towards her brother. Skeletal ribs loomed like ivory pillars as she struggled among them, clawing determinedly towards the ruined shape.

Niklos was still alive when she reached him. He smiled hopefully, as if he might steal her away to the stars. 'See, Dai?' He caressed her face with a bloodied hand. 'It all comes to nothing in the end.' He faded, his last breath dissipating into the wind.

An inferno blew through Daimonia's flesh. Her trembling hands reached for Niklos' sword as if compelled. Her fingers tightened with a force she had never mustered and she gripped it as might an assassin. A dark potency filled her and she practised some quick thrusts, exhaling hard with each stab. *Have I strength enough to pierce flesh and kill?*

The crowd had fallen to a hush. Prettanike's lips were drawn into a thin contemptuous smile.

Daimonia felt time slow as she rushed at the Executioner. Her feet kicked up sand as they ploughed into the ground, launching her forwards. She was unleashed, every muscle singing as she forced herself at Prettanike, a stab aimed at her enemy's throat.

The blade touched the Executioner's neck, steel kissing flesh for a moment. Prettanike's leg shot out, her powerful kick destroying Daimonia with a snap.

Daimonia teetered with pain as an ache erupted from the depths of her stomach and branched up through her chest. Her fingertips were numb and her mouth full of sick. Disorientated, she fell to bite the filthy sand.

A single droplet of blood eased from the graze at Prettanike's throat. It rolled gleaming down her tanned skin, an affront to the gladiator's prowess.

May one drop of blood become a river, Daimonia prayed. She rolled onto her back, staring at the sea of faces above.

The crowd were screaming with laughter. Men threw themselves into the pit to raise Prettanike on their shoulders or else rejoice as if the victory had been their own. They raised triumphant fists to the sun.

The Bloody Crossroads

In a tavern at Littlecrook, a wobbly yeoman gave his distinct rendition of events. 'I saw it clear as the nose on my face. A girl jumped into the Meat Pit, killed all the Knight Executioners and then chopped off the baron's cock!'

'Clearly you weren't even there,' a balding knight contradicted the first account. 'I saw the whole thing and the girl clearly jumped down shouting, "For the women!" She was then immediately martyred.'

'Maybe it was the Goddess,' the bartender offered with a gulp. 'The girl was slaughtered by Prettanike, but her body mysteriously disappeared.'

'Either way it was the worst fight I ever saw,' a squinting elder complained. 'So one-sided! Just once I'd like to see someone take on insurmountable odds and, not just win, but literally swim in the blood of their enemies!'

'They chopped that boy up after Prettanike was done with him,' the bartender continued. 'Hung him up with the other traitors at the crossroads.'

'I'd have done exactly the same thing.' The bald knight slapped the table. 'I hear he was fiddling with kiddies!' He recoiled at the thought, as if someone had waved dung in his face. 'Leave him for the maggots!

That's what I say!'

As the debate declined into chatter, a pair of shadows arose from the corner and quietly departed.

Daimonia's eyes were wide with trepidation as she stared into the shameless night. She was braced to see the truth, no matter how terrible it might be. Fleeing in the rickety horse-drawn cart, the girl hugged her aching body, watching locks of windy hair play around her face.

The horse's reins were guided by Jhonan's trembling hands. The old man's face was limp and corpselike, but his eyes burned when the crossroads came into sight.

The Leechfinger crossroads was a grotesque forest of crow-pecked bodies. Six men hung crudely nailed to tree and post, stripped and brutally mutilated. Each haggard face was twisted in fear and anger, an exhibition of rotted teeth, bulging eyes and blood-thick beards. Their last thoughts had been swarming with palpable hate.

A glorious tapestry of stars gleamed upon this arrangement of death, illuminating the faces with such sharp shadow and light that they seemed noble as statues. One oddly tranquil face could be found amongst the dead. The serene expression belonged to Niklos. The starlight enshrined his body, revealing stumps where his legs had been.

At the sight of her dismembered brother, Daimonia felt her heart die. *Is there a stronger version of me who can survive this moment?*

Two mounted road-watchmen approached. They were dressed in weather-beaten greatcoats, with long-necked spurs on their boots. One watchman wore a thick leather face guard revealing nothing but predatory eyes glaring into the night. The other was ghastly thin and suffered from horribly ulcerated cheeks and self-inflicted facial scratches. Both men had the hungry stare of opportunists.

Daimonia brimmed with hate at the sight of these agents of the baron. She made the sign of Cere-Thalatte to protect herself from their greed. If the riders were offended by the insulting gesture, they hid it well behind their insatiable stares.

Jhonan gave the barest nod to the night-watchmen as he stopped the cart by the hanging bodies.

'Wotcha doing, you dirty old pig?' the masked watchman demanded. 'Thieving trinkets from the dead?'

Jhonan wearily raised his empty hands to show he meant no provocation. The old man's palms were as scarred as war-worn axe-heads. 'I claim the body of my grandson Niklos. We are taking him home for the adjurator to perform the last rites.' Jhonan dismounted and stood ready by the corpse.

In the cart Daimonia touched her pallid face with her hands. She searched the watchmen's expressions for something other than cruelty but found them lacking. A sound of despair escaped from her lips.

'Each of 'em was a dirty traitor,' the masked watchman gloated. 'The dead stay where they are, as a warning to others.'

'He's paid for his crime,' Jhonan reasoned. 'Surely no further payment can be taken than his life? He needs to come home for the proper rites.'

'Oh, we'll all be paying more before long,' the ulcerated watchman commiserated while picking absently at his face. 'Mate of mine from

49

Kraljevic reckons the prince needs more silver for the endless bloody war. You know what that means? More bleedin' taxes. But as for the dead lad, how about we turn a blind eye to him vanishing and you leave us your horse?'

'Plainly I can't part with the horse.' Jhonan looked exasperated at the negotiation. 'You watchmen ought to show some mercy. Your guild is hated enough by anyone who must use these roads. Why add cruelty to shameless greed?'

'Strikes me your girl could sweeten the deal,' the watchman suggested, completely unabashed by the chastisement. His fidgety picking finger had moved to his blistered ear and was thrusting inside searchingly.

'I'm unimpressed by your threats,' Jhonan replied steadily. 'I'm taking my grandson home and you'd best let me get to it.'

'Not happening,' the masked watchman decided. 'The body stays right where it's put.'

The old man broke up then. Tears singed his eyes and he buried his face into his forearm. The riders glanced at each other, taken aback by the sudden show of emotion.

An arrow struck into the head of the masked watchman. The penetration was no deeper than the arrowhead and instead of dying the watchman pawed stupidly at his face and fell sideways out of his saddle.

Daimonia drew another arrow from her quiver and aimed at the second rider. The meandering wind, now cold and decisive, billowed around her hair and cloak approvingly.

The split second of silence that followed became a deafening roar. A lion unleashed, Jhonan leapt for the panicking scab-faced watchman, who was petrified by his own excitement.

They hit the floor rolling and struggling, both men attempting to wrest fatal advantage over the other. As the gap in their prowess became quickly evident, the air was filled with Jhonan's derisive laughter. Mocking the watchman's desperation, he wrenched a hammer-headed pick from his leather belt. The old man rose above his inferior opponent and waited a full moment before delivering two heavy blows that shattered the scabby face.

The other watchman was not yet dead. Jhonan cut that one's throat with the brutal efficiency of a butcher. As the watchman gargled and spat, Daimonia was both appalled and fascinated by the violence she had instigated.

Jhonan wiped his bloody hands on his cloak and spat upon the ground. He guided one of the watchmen's horses back to his own cart and tethered it. The other rider's horse had bolted terrified into the night. Jhonan then relieved both dead watchmen of their coin. Each action led to the next, as natural as pissing.

When Jhonan's attention returned to his grandson's body, he finally gave pause. His brow furrowed and he bit at his crusted lip. Looking back at his granddaughter in the cart, he scowled to see her trembling uselessly.

'Dai!' Jhonan shouted at the shaking girl. 'Help me with your brother's body.'

'Grandfather, I cannot do it.'

'You must.'

The Geld Knight's Tax

Geld Knight Conrad Ernst arrived at dawn, riding with an expression of grandiose importance. His face was turned away from the sun, allowing his obsessively combed hair to become a crown of reflected light. Across his shoulders he wore an ambitiously colourful cloak fastened with a carnelian brooch. His cuirass was painted gold and shaped to pretend a heroically muscled torso.

'So this is Jaromir, men.' The words seemed to come through his nose. 'I suggest you find food, ale and some tail.'

Conrad entered the muddy village, steering his horse ahead of the armed enforcers who trudged behind him. His men were not regular militants or conscripted soldiers; rather they were criminals hand-picked for their intimidating looks and lack of scruples. Some had been pressed into service rather than meeting death in the Meat Pit, saved by little more than their ugliness. Following the knight, these Geld enforcers hungrily surveyed the villagers, who halted work to stare at the unsavoury men.

'Sir Conrad,' one of the enforcers yelled, 'I saw the fat one first!'

The Geld Knight turned to watch a hearty-looking chit among the staring women, who blushed at the lecherous attention of the enforcers. Conrad's men all laughed as she ran to her husband, a miller who looked as red-faced and cowed as she did.

Fotter, the rabbit-toothed trapper, made some moaning noises. There was more lascivious laughter.

The Geld Knight toyed with the steel codpiece that generously emphasised his genitals. His ringed fingers lingered over the armoured phallus that curled upwards and was crowned with the impression of a grinning moustached face. It was a magnificent gleaming protrusion, but his crotch ached mercilessly within it.

'Duty first for us, old man,' Conrad told the face.

The gawking peasants were waiting. 'All taxes must be presented at the shire hall by midday,' Conrad told them sharply. 'Including your donations for the untiring crusade of Sir John-Richard-Paul.' He allowed himself a smug grin. The only crusading Sir John-Richard-Paul undertook was to the most extravagant taverns and disreputable whorehouses. Still, even that required plenty of money.

Trained as a political apologist, Conrad enjoyed the subtleties of distorting language, paradoxical statements and corruptions of meaning. In the academy the methods had been presented as a sacred art, a means to protect the prince and the Accord. Conrad knew that claim was itself a distortion. Apologists made truth elusive and portrayed wicked deeds as righteous. They authored lies so that people would obey. Was it really necessary to add self-deception to that mandate?

In idle summers at the royal courts of Kraljevic, Conrad had used the art to seduce the wives of men he admired or envied. The fleeting memory of those warm and selfish nights drove Conrad's hand back to the armoured protrusion at his crotch.

No lover compared to the wife of Pavel, Conrad's mentor. Elena-Beleka was a distinguished woman, with a hedonistic reputation that made many men cower in her presence. She discovered Conrad in the busy cloisters where the prince's ministers whispered conspiratorially. Kissing Conrad's hand, Elena-Beleka had drawn the young man into the dark, making a bed of every shadow. Conrad had pursued her like a hapless boy, ruining his fortune on gifts to woo the insatiable woman.

A sweaty gush poured from Conrad's brow and he struggled to adjust his armour. Since being appointed to the Charitable Order of Geld Collectors, Conrad was authorised to collect meat in all its forms. But the offerings were dreary and Conrad's appetite could only be appeased by old memories.

Conrad mused that beauty in the villages was rarer than an act of honesty in the cities. The women were too headstrong and rarely more attractive than the livestock. Nevertheless Fotter was already giving playful chase to the meagre beauty on offer. Conrad knew he would have to conduct the prince's business swiftly or end up with the absolute dregs, which typically meant bedding someone's grandmother. He set towards the shire hall, absently wetting his lips.

As the dawn light succumbed to encroaching clouds, the Geld

enforcers helped themselves to food and a squeeze of tit. The village at least was busy with life and purpose. Chickens scattered from the approach of mangy dogs. Orphans from the Chapel of Life upset a cart and ran off jeering. Ravens patrolled the treetops.

Within the shire hall a collection of candles burned fretfully. A musty stench reeked from the deteriorated timber. An old greyhound lay with its head low, as if waiting for the ceiling to collapse. Beside the dog sat Scir Wendel shaking his gaunt head wearily. He anxiously thumbed through the tax ledger. Any discrepancy might lead to a humiliating punishment.

Conrad pictured the mask he would wear for this engagement. He formed its contours in his mind before moulding his features into the appropriate look. The first moment was important, laying the foundation for the outcome. Conrad took pride in doing things well, even with such a dull victim to work on.

'Dark times,' he boomed from the shadows.

'Sir Conrad!' The old scir shrivelled at the Geld Knight's presence. 'I was just making everything ready for your inspection.' Wendel wrenched himself up and performed a crooked bow.

Conrad sat himself in the scir's chair and rifled idly through the ledger. 'You seem to have come up short.'

'Times are always difficult, my lord. We have this season sent many more sons to the garrison and…'

'We will settle the balance later.' Conrad waved away the scir's chattering. 'We first must discuss these Knights Anarchist who have been murdering Seidhr workers and strangling agents of the baron.'

'Knights Anarchist?' Scir Wendell looked horrified. 'I've never even heard of–'

'Yes, it was the prince himself who first coined the phrase. Knights Anarchist, the prince said, are the most insidious of all criminals. When a man takes it upon himself to undermine the very society that gave him status and rank' – Conrad imitated Prince Moranion's noble gestures – 'such revolt constitutes the highest form of treason against the Accord!'

'You think such men will come to Jaromir?' Wendel looked deliciously afeared, his eyes ringed with wrinkles. Between the horrifying threat of Baoth raiders and the never-ending war against the False Prince, these people could be scared into paying any price to feel safe.

'Perhaps they are here already,' Conrad replied cryptically.

'Goddess preserve us!' Wendel exclaimed. 'We only have two militants stationed here, and one of them is even more elderly than I am!'

Conrad winced at the exclamation. He hated the goddess. It was absurd that an imaginary power was considered greater than the princedom by these superstitious peasants.

'Calm yourself,' he demanded. 'Many of these traitor knights have already been caught and crucified. Even now they hang at the Leechfinger crossroads, a warning to all betrayers. Unfortunately for you one of them came from Jaromir, which means the entire village incurs a proxy tax for treason.'

'Proxy what?' A new kind of terror had filled the old man's face. Not the abstract fear of foreign invaders, but the sensation of sinking helplessly into the Geld Knight's manipulations.

'Niklos Vornir; his family reside here, do they not?'

'Young Niklos a traitor? I can't believe that, my lord. I've never known a better boy!'

'You've enjoyed a relationship with this criminal?'

'What? No, my lord. I'm not party to anything. Least of all that.'

'His family.' Conrad stood and tapped the ledgers with an insistent finger.

Wendel wrung his frail hands. 'Old Jhonan Vornir lives in the watchtower with his granddaughter, Daimonia. He's a miserable old bastard, though. I wouldn't go up there.'

'Granddaughter, you say.' Conrad raised a golden eyebrow. The ache was beginning to return. 'Is the girl fair?'

'What?'

'You heard me. Is the girl fair?'

'Well, she's a spirited girl, clever. But young, barely a woman.'

Conrad caressed the grinning face on his codpiece. 'Then I will take her as payment for the corruption that has been allowed to breed in this disgusting immoral place.'

'Take Daimonia?' The scir whimpered, but the Geld Knight was already taking his leave.

Halting by the timid candles, Conrad took a moment to bask in the power of his will. He let out a little gasp of joy, savouring the extraordinary gold of his soul. With sudden delight Conrad noticed the flames dancing as if to a regal symphony. He could hear the grand music that moved them; it was so familiar he might have composed it himself.

Conrad laughed as the flames became little people dancing so very politely for his amusement, little people bowing in obeisance to his greatness.

Ceresoph Unearthed

The dead girl was hidden beneath the earth, her wooden face blemished by mud and stone. She had been silent in the darkness for years, her lips just a tiny indenture on her weathered face. Beside the old stones and crawling things, she had lain afraid to move.

'Wake up, Cere.'

Daimonia excavated the thing with her hands, cupping the sad doll in her palm and cleaning it with her sleeve. The wooden girl was a little smaller than her forearm and had no discernible arms or legs. It had once enjoyed wild woollen hair but was now bald and hatless. Daimonia rubbed at its mud-smeared cheeks and then looked the thing in the eye.

'I bid you awaken.'

Running her thumb over the doll's tiny nose, Daimonia recalled how she had buried the doll along with every part of herself that had made her mother leave.

'Your questions are a plague,' Lady Catherine had often scolded her. 'How can I have birthed such an uncertain thing as you?'

Daimonia caught herself reciting those stinging words to Cere, who absorbed them with the same wooden calm she did everything. Perhaps inside the doll was crying or bleeding, even screaming to the stars. Was she yearning for a love she would never know?

'Our brother is dead,' Daimonia told the doll in a childish voice. 'He didn't believe in the Accord anymore. He discovered too many dirty secrets. Did you creep from the earth and infect him with your doubts? I should burn you 'til you confess.'

Daimonia shuddered recalling the madness of the haunted journey back to Jaromir. She had tried to resurrect Niklos with her kisses, but the dead boy had only stared serenely at the stars. The brilliant sea of light above them was awash with waves of jade and azure light, the enthroned souls of all who passed before. Gleaming brightest among them all was the Eye of Ceresoph from whence all life sprang.

'Remember me on your burning flight,' Daimonia had pleaded, imagining Niklos' soul returning to the luminous mother. She had sought his brightness in the sky when a sound had erupted like terrible laughter. Jhonan's harsh sobs had frightened and surprised her. She had hugged Niklos' cold body to calm her terrified breathing.

Darkness fell upon the garden and Daimonia released a haunted gasp.

'What are you doing, Dai?' Jhonan was blocking the sun, his wild brows knotted in consternation. His arms, thick with old war muscle, looked ready to lash out as they had so many times at young Niklos. He wore his favourite military boots and no toil could wear them thin. After all he had seen, the man was still substantial and unconquerable.

'Nothing,' Daimonia replied distantly. She pouted like a much younger girl, imitating the age she had been when she first buried Cere.

Jhonan crouched and took Cere from Daimonia's hand, turning the doll over with his best fingers. 'The adjurators are preparing Nik for the burning tomorrow.'

'I'm going to steal back the years.' Daimonia snatched the doll and held it up as if speaking for it. 'Back to when we were all together. And if anyone tries to leave, I'll kill myself!'

'Dai, you're not yourself.'

'Not myself?'

Jhonan chased a vague fear with his eyes. 'The shadow of things I've done falls over all our family,' he said heavily. 'May you always be unlike me.'

'I'm not like you!' Daimonia was inflamed, her voice going from child to vengeful Goddess. 'My hands are not drenched in blood like a murderer's!' For a moment she glimpsed the potential depths of her anger and felt terrified by her own proclivity for hate. The bare hurt in the old man's eyes drew her back from the edge.

She fled to her room, where the shutters were wide open to the sun. To the east stood a lonely tree, at which Daimonia had often lingered, longing for someone to love. In the surrounding woods she and Niklos used to imitate their mother's adventures, recreating a hundred imaginary battles. Daimonia would pretend to be Lady Catherine, slaying cannibalistic raiders and defying scheming rebels. Niklos would play a variety of famous heroes, from Sir John-Richard-Paul to Prince Moranion. Sticks became swords and hapless sheep were sometimes cast as outlaws or lurking horrors from Archonian times.

In those games their mother had represented the champion of stability and order. She fought against everything that was foreign and uncertain. Even in her absence Lady Catherine was potent and present.

Each night, stern Jhonan had called them in for sleep. How they feared their grandfather, who had once been a famous knight and was regarded with dread by every man who knew his name. Jhonan would tell them that family was the most important thing in the world, and each night the children would cry themselves to sleep.

Daimonia slammed the shutters closed on the memory and retreated to her bed.

She curled up and held herself, her mind both feeding and fighting her fears. She allowed the contest in the Meat Pit to repeat in her mind. Saw Niklos' gentle face becoming weak with fear and pain, his lips trembling with horror and regret as Prettanike humiliated him. She could taste the tears that flooded his dying smile.

Daimonia's long fingers clasped the old bedposts and her body stiffened, racked by uncontrollably furious breaths. 'It cannot be so.' Her mind reeled, incredulous at her own violent recollections. She could still hear Niklos' testimony, the abuses he had witnessed and the terrible murder he had confessed. Trial by combat had been his stubborn choice, but would any route have led to a different fate? Execution was the end of all who defied the Accord, and who would credit a lowly knight over Seidhr and lords?

What am I to do? Daimonia despaired. *I am not a knight or noble. My only weapons are questions.*

'Goddess, I am weak!' she raged.

Across the room the stone bust of Daimonia's mother witnessed this outburst with disapproval. The white face seemed alive with haughty

62

disdain.

Daimonia sat bolt upright to meet the statue's glare, her skin tingling with a ghostly veil of sweat. She emerged from the bed, fixated on the condescending expression. Never had the statue seemed so real an approximation of Lady Catherine's contempt.

Daimonia's hand mirror made a good weapon for striking repeatedly at the stone.

'Why weren't you here?' Daimonia shattered the glass against the imperious face. 'They would've listened to you!'

A constellation of tiny glinting shards were cast around the room. Several larger pieces were wedged into the girl's fingers. She bit her lip and began tearing them free as the blood rushed down her hand. The physical pain was inconsequential compared to the rebellion within. Daimonia watched the scarlet run down her arm with a macabre fascination.

A rising tumult of voices was encroaching from the village and Daimonia peered through the shutters to see the cause.

From Jaromir a great procession was marching towards Vornir Manor. Among them was Scir Wendell, who was almost dripping with anxiety, shaking his head and biting his knuckles. Daimonia allowed herself a short laugh; the old scir was such a worrier.

Most of the village adults were among the crowd, as well as the chapel orphans, who seized any opportunity for mischief. There were strangers among the crowd too, but Daimonia recognised their look. They were friends to violence and drink, men like her grandfather who wore their guilt with pride. She aimed at each killer with her bloody finger, noticing first a huge unfortunate misfit enjoying the camaraderie of the mean. She spied a leering hunter replete with the skins of his kills. She pointed to a well-travelled Afreyan grinning as if his fortune was one more murder away. With the most contempt she spotted a half-witted youth who aspired to be like these animals.

Are they here for Jhonan? Perhaps these were old enemies, walking grudges from a violent past. *If they kill him, I too will die,* she decided.

Emerging at the front, an extraordinary figure caught Daimonia's full attention. The golden knight had a sense of consequence and purpose as he strode ahead of the crowd. He was surprisingly handsome, gifted with luminous hair and strength of jaw and brow. Across his shoulders he wore the most fabulous cloak the girl had ever seen, a playful rainbow of exotic colours and shades. Daimonia held her breath at the sight of him – a thing of myth walking into her life.

The Dispute

The whole village had flocked around the Geld Knight and his enforcers by the time they had climbed the hill to the Vornir place. Sir Conrad was bemused at what all the peasants found so thrilling about the old tottering tower. Nevertheless every hare-brained idiot was gleefully tagging along for the occasion. Hopefully the girl would be worth the fuss.

'What do you make of it, Fotter?' Conrad often spoke to his subordinates without looking at them squarely. He tipped his head back and glanced down his nose imperiously, just as he'd been taught at the academy.

'I dunno. But I can sniff out a pretty one.' Fotter snorted, slapping Conrad on the back. 'Maybe I can have a go on her too?' He followed up the suggestion with some farmyard noises.

Men of low character used vulgar talk as a means of bonding, assuring themselves that each was as damaged as the other. Conrad indulged them for the most part, but these men could never think of him as their friend. Friends were for betraying.

Conrad wrenched the trapper's lank hair, pulling Fotter's ear to his mouth. 'Try to remember that we are the law,' he scolded, twisting the greasy locks.

'Sorry, sir.'

Conrad had collected many things as taxes, little of which ever made it back to Kraljevic. There was an abundance of silver, livestock and sexual acts on offer. But beyond those mundane transactions Conrad was building a little empire of his own within the south, claiming property, land and militia. He was accumulating his own small sovereignty. But when the ache was painful, only a girl would do, and when the Accord had been betrayed, a strong display of discipline was essential.

As Conrad and his men reached the crumbling place, a figure emerged tentatively from the tower's gloomy alcoves. Hesitant to face the crowd, she lingered by the tenebrous vines.

'That's Daimonia, my lord.' Scir Wendel's voice was pathetic with regret.

'Come forward, girl,' Conrad commanded.

The girl emerged, all hair and unconscious womanhood, and stood wondering at the sight of the gathering. It was easy to see she was healthy and of good stock, but more than that she appeared curious and interested.

The Afreyan mercenary grinned approvingly. 'In my homeland we call such girls *little fish*,' he told Sir Conrad.

'I'd stuff 'er,' the brutish Cain added bluntly.

'Quiet, men!' Conrad was reminded of the goddess statues in Kraljevic: implausible beauty in the form of youth, mother or destroyer. But the ancient artists had no sweeter muse than this one and a sweat of desire flooded his crotch, lust threatening to destroy his command of the moment. He calmed himself; she was his for the taking. He need only will it so.

The crowd began chattering loudly, inexplicably enlivened by a second presence stalking out from the tower. Although visibly drunk, this old wretch presented himself with firm confidence, glaring at the villagers, who nodded in fearful deference. His scowling black brows were perhaps something to be avoided.

Conrad found the old a horrible generation. The elderly had an acute awareness of their own entitlements and a morbid attention to the manners of others. Conrad predicted a loud outburst of some sort before the girl would be handed over.

'You,' he told the old man. 'Your name is Vornir?'

The old man levelled an accusatory look at the crowd. This was too much for some who turned and walked away. No doubt they knew better than to antagonise a raging drunk.

'I am Jhonan Vornir.' The old man's voice was substantial and resonant. 'As everyone here can attest.' He glared again at the villagers, who seemed entranced by the whole performance.

'By the authority of the Geld,' Conrad declared, noting how nasal his own voice was by comparison. 'I enforce a proxy tax for the treason of your grandson, Niklos Vornir. I hereby claim your granddaughter as my property. She will become a servant of the Geld for as long as I see fit.'

The old man looked completely unfazed by the announcement and it dawned on Conrad that the senile fool had not understood it.

'That girl' – Conrad pointed violently – 'belongs to me now.'

'As a Knight of the Accord, I assert my right to dispute your claim by combat.'

There was a great swell of noise and laughter from the crowd. Some threw their hats in the air. The idiots were cheering the old fool on and revelling in his defiance. Conrad realised their interest in this affair was to see an old man slaughtered. It was understandable. There was no appeasing the desire for bloody spectacle among the powerless. Such things gave them an illusory rush of potency.

'So granted.' Conrad suffered the old knight's request.

'I'll kill him,' offered the eager youth Scorcher. The youngest enforcer was keen to please but had precious little decorum.

'No, I will,' Conrad decided.

Daimonia had been sent to the tower but now returned hefting an archaic sword and a mail shirt, with which she prepared her grandfather for battle. It struck Conrad as a strange moment. She neither pleaded nor wept, but almost with relish dressed her grandfather for death.

'I like this girl,' Conrad told himself. The moment held a fascinating innocence. It reminded him of the old poem:

No one spoke to the old man
Once his wife had died
Only a child, strange with grief
Echoed lost beauty at his side.

Where had he heard that? He remembered his fair sister singing in the golden fields as a child. They had filled those summer afternoons with a wealth of songs and tales, Isabelle's voice rich with naive joy. The recollection was warming, a brief radiance from the time before their parents' death. Conrad sniffed. A melancholy had snuck up on him,

68

making him whimper involuntarily. How old would Isabelle be now?

'Are you all right, Sir Conrad?'

'Of course I'm alright, Fotter.' Conrad wiped innocuously at his eye, recovering himself. 'Is the old man ready yet?'

Ravens circled overhead, quietly soaring around the tower.

Jhonan stepped forth and saluted with his sword. The old man looked as if he were already dead, but he was ready to fight anyway. In his left hand he held a jagged dagger pointed away from Conrad. Ceremonial details were clearly of great significance to the retired knight, but Conrad merely tipped his head in slight acknowledgement.

The crowd fell quiet once the preparations were done. They had formed a semicircle around the killing ground and a look of fevered anticipation filled each stupid face.

The enemies closed in on each other, circling carefully for the first opening. Despite the infirmity of his opponent, Conrad felt a rush of trepidation excite his body. His face burned and his heart raced involuntarily. It belatedly occurred to him how the formal duels of the academy were his only direct experience of combat. He had performed adequately in that arena, albeit often by deceit. Nevertheless, the old knight was best put down quickly.

Jhonan Vornir was smiling as he circled with sword and dagger. He looked as if about to cut up and eat his dinner. Vornir's confidence made Conrad hate him and want to see those hard eyes weeping blood.

With a rush Conrad lunged at his enemy. His form was excellent and the piercing blow would have driven through a horse. But Jhonan was at his side, stabbing swiftly at Conrad's unprotected armpit with his dagger.

Conrad ripped himself away, convulsing at the galling pain and the tremendous amount of blood let loose.

Cheers rose among the villagers. Their local bastard had almost ended the fight with a single blow. Conrad seethed at the crowd's excitement, feeling mocked by their pleasure. It dawned on him that they expected Jhonan to win and blatantly wanted to see the Geld humiliated.

With roaring rage he ran at Jhonan, hacking and stabbing. The excruciating soreness in his armpit made each thrust agony, but the pain spurred him on. The Geld Enforcers cheered with cries of 'come on, Sir Conrad' and 'gut 'im!'

Sir Conrad was wasting himself in his temper. Jhonan backed away, parried then rushed in again. The Geld Knight's shield intercepted the attempt, slamming the old face with a satisfying crunch. Vornir staggered back spitting teeth. Conrad pressed the moment; he chopped at Jhonan's neck, but a hefty parry met the strike. The swords clanged apart with a shudder.

A swift kick caught the old fool, but Jhonan seized Conrad's ankle and dragged him hopping through the slushy muck. The crowd laughed raucously.

Conrad caught himself trying to smirk away his own awkward predicament. *A momentary setback*, his expression seemed to say. *A crowd-pleasing amusement before I piss all over the old man's corpse.*

The enforcers were visibly appalled at the ignominious state of their illustrious leader. They were bristling to get stuck in, desperate to cut Jhonan down themselves.

Sweat drenched Conrad's brow. He wrenched his foot free, falling flat on his back. Mud spattered everywhere. He recovered quickly, trying to remember the old tricks. He pretended to drop his weapon, but Jhonan did not take the bait. He feigned a retreat, but his enemy would not be fooled. The Geld Knight's courage was being eroded by the old man's wolfish cunning. The truth of it was plain: Jhonan Vornir was a raven of war, a true killer who meant to wear him down and destroy him.

Jhonan charged, forcing the Geld Knight to slide uncertainly in the mud. The old man broke through sword range and hacked again with the accursed dagger. Conrad lost his sword and attempted to stem the attack with a grapple.

The clamouring voices mocked Conrad's predicament as the fighters wrestled furiously. He glimpsed their jeering faces and wanted to stamp on each one.

Locked in intimate combat, the men snarled and spat at each other. Such close quarters were terrain Conrad knew well, but Vornir's strength was oppressive. Conrad felt a flash of gratification as he swept Jhonan's ankle and sent the bastard toppling haphazardly. Before the old man could recover his weapons, Conrad was on him, squeezing the strong old neck, forcing wheezing breaths from the warrior's throat.

'Now you die, you old relic!' Conrad's eyes were bulging with madness. 'Join your grandson among the traitorous dead, for all to spit upon and despise.'

Jhonan Vornir was growling and gasping. He had too few full fingers to break the strangulating grasp. His face boiled red and he sank his irregular teeth into Conrad's wrist with a gnashing, chewing spite. Conrad staggered away, his face aghast with an excess of pain.

Jhonan struggled after him, his beard thick with sweat and slivers of flesh. He dragged Conrad down, pressed the Geld Knight's head into the muck and knelt on it. Forcing his hand up under the illustrious codpiece, he grasped Conrad's testicles. Clenching with abrupt strength, he crushed his hand into a fist. Conrad pleaded, but there were no cunning words that would overcome Vornir. This was a master of violence and cruelty.

Suffocating in waves of excruciating pain, Conrad began to fade from the moment. His body jarred as his mind fell into the stained pit of memory.

Orphaned as a child, Conrad had been separated from his sister to become an initiate at the Exalt Temple. He had been a beautiful boy then, although that innocence seemed a stranger now. He had dreamed of becoming an adjurator and administering all the rituals of life.

One night while bathing, he had been stroked and probed by the High Adjurator, cupped by those cold and veiny hands. 'You are the one,' the Adjurator had croaked, 'the special one.' Yearning to be loved, Conrad had surrendered his will to the powerful old man.

The following years had been humiliating and dark. The High Adjurator was insatiable and cruel whilst regarded as saintly and benevolent. He stripped the boy of all dignity and taught him what it was to be utterly at the mercy of another's power. But the terror of this subjection produced a revelation.

The intimate encounters confirmed Conrad's conviction that he was

72

indeed special, a favourite of sorts and better than others. He was convinced that in the end everyone would come to understand his superiority in some profound way. His fellow students at the academy had laughed when he tried to explain it to them. But Conrad knew the truth. There was a Secret God, never spoken of by the priests, who would revenge every slight and injury.

He returned to his pain as the villagers of Jaromir became a cheering, roaring army, an overwhelming force riding on the back of Vornir's triumph.

'You leave Jaromir now.' Jhonan's dominance had made a subjugated boy of Conrad again. 'Taking not a whit more than is owed you.'

Voices from the Dust

'The dead teach us all things,' Adjurator Ivan told the village mourners with practised solemnity. 'They teach us the future and the past. They teach us how to live and how to die.'

Daimonia had heard this recitation many times; death was common as birds in Jaromir. The coast was beset by Baoth raiders and war loomed for young men recruited to the garrison. Mothers often died in childbirth, children rarely lived beyond infancy, and the infirm were claimed each winter. Now death had seized her brother too.

Every member of the community was present, with one notable exception. Jhonan had been drinking constantly since his duel with the Geld Knight and Daimonia had been forced to leave him and come alone. Nevertheless the fight had enlivened the villagers, reminding them of the power of resistance. Perhaps they were all just a little more stubborn, ever since the night of the inspiring play.

The adjurators had cleaned and dressed her brother for the burning. These were men of the Order of Life, husbands of the Goddess, who lived in a chapel with the local orphans. The adjurators administered all village rituals: the rites of birth, marriage and death.

Despite the adjurators' best efforts, Niklos looked like a badly made effigy of himself. His body was a husk devoid of kindness, arrogance or foolish bravery. Whatever the essential Niklos was, it was absent from this flesh.

As they carried her brother to the pyre, Daimonia wondered if she too were dead. Her skin was stone pale and she shivered with a nightmarish chill. Her eyes were frozen and tearless, seeing everything yet nothing. Her feelings had become elusive, glimpsed imperfectly through fractured ice.

Even travellers mourned with the community as if the loss were their own. *If strangers can weep at the sight of my dead brother, then why can't I who loved him?*

Niklos was laid down and a torch-bearer stood forth, ready to ignite the pyre. An orphan had been chosen for the honour, a strange youth whose mind was broken. Villiam the Fool was bigger and older than Daimonia but would never be able to leave the adjurators' care as he was too dangerous to look after himself.

Villiam wore a crooked smile as he put the torch to the kindling. He was so proud to be helping that he shook his fist in triumph when the pyre took flame. Some of the villagers scowled at his impiety, but Daimonia kissed him on the cheek.

'Thank you, Villiam,' she whispered.

'I will be your brother now,' he declared innocently.

Daimonia let out a surprised laugh. Villiam had sometimes nuisanced her grandfather by imitating Jhonan's gruff mannerisms and following him around the village. She wondered if there was something of the divine in his play.

Adjurator Ivan put a gentle hand on the boy's shoulder. 'Come along,

Villiam,' he encouraged. 'Leave Daimonia be.'

The boy went compliantly, his face rearranging into a faraway stare that better suited a wise man than a fool.

With all her heart Daimonia longed to see her mother here. Closing her eyes, she imagined the resolute woman stood among the mourners in her impenetrable armour. How magnificent and untouchable she would try to be, her chin lifted high with pride, brandishing the impervious expression of a Knight of the Accord. Or would she be broken, wailing and screaming at the body of her dead son? Would she be devastated at having ever left her children?

Daimonia caught herself clawing at her own arm in agitation, a habit she had long been rid of. Then came the moment she was anticipating with curiosity and dread. Adjurator Ivan made the sign of the star as he began the ritual. He stared directly at Daimonia with the merest suggestion of a smile. Then with a slow intake of breath, he closed his eyes and his face became completely relaxed, vacant of any expression. When he next spoke, his voice took on gentle tones that approximated those of her dead brother.

'I came into the world without fear and I leave it the same way,' Adjurator Ivan began, speaking for Niklos by the power of the Goddess. 'To my family and friends I wish a life as free as my own.'

The channelling complete, Adjurator Ivan blinked and seemed to become himself again.

'Niklos' soul has passed to Mother Cerenox,' old Frater Moss announced dutifully. He had recorded the adjurator's sayings in the Book of Dead Words.

Is that all? Daimonia wondered. Niklos' last words seemed trite and vaguely familiar, like an old adage. There was no mention of Niklos' turmoil with the Accord. There were no special words for Daimonia, nor hint of the childhood secrets they had shared. There were no words for their absent mother.

Daimonia eyed the adjurators sharply and wondered whether the whole Order of Life was a sham. Frater Moss was old and miserable, but Adjurator Ivan's expression was so open she found it hard to imagine him with anything but the kindest intentions. Observing the gathered community with curiosity, she gauged their credulity. From venerable Scir Wendel to the youngest child, everyone had a look of satisfied trust.

Villiam the Fool had wandered from the crowd and fallen; Daimonia saw his terrible writhing shape and ran over hurriedly. Villiam convulsed horribly in the thick mud, his broad shoulders twisting and his legs kicking violently against the earth. His mouth was wide with an unspoken scream, mucus drizzling from his nose. He spread his fingers like the tips of a crown around his head.

Daimonia approached cautiously. She was aware that the Goddess sometimes troubled Villiam and it was best to make sure he didn't hurt himself. But he was saying something, forcing out words in a familiar voice.

Daimonia drew closer, careful not to be struck by the lashing of Villiam's arms and legs. She observed his neck straining, his head turning towards her with painful effort. Seeing her, Villiam's face became earnest.

'I will be avenged a thousandfold,' he vowed.

It was the voice of her brother.

A raven broke abruptly from the trees and took flight, circling the mourners. Black wings against grey sky. The raven glided toward Vornir Manor, where shadows suggested skull-like hollows amid the decaying stone.

Within those sepulchral walls old Jhonan crawled drunkenly towards the fire, clinging to the stone as if he might fall from the floor. The warrior had made a fiery memorial of his grandson's old possessions: a Book of the Accord, a birth-rite bell and a wooden training sword. He spat and snarled at the flame, seeming poised to throw himself in it.

Jhonan cursed the Goddess and plunged his hand into the fire, searing his own flesh. Her shadow fell upon him as he roared and clenched his fist against his chest. He trembled and shrank from the dreadful figure, recoiling from her vindictive presence.

'Niklos will be avenged,' she told him coldly.

'No, Daimonia,' the old man protested. His voice was as raw as a wound. 'No, we bury our grievance with Nik.'

'We are Vornirs and we will avenge.'

Jhonan rose unsteadily to his feet, trying to gather his authority. The fire made a foolish silhouette of his swaying drunken shape. 'We took two lives for the one that was lost to us,' he reasoned desperately.

'Our true grievance is with the baron,' Daimonia asserted. 'Let no other blood placate us.'

'Nik was a traitor!' Jhonan flared, brandishing his sword as if he would have killed the boy himself. 'Will you join your brother nailed to a tree? Or perhaps you would prefer to be banished to the depths of

Archonia?'

'Yes. I would sooner betray the prince than my own brother.'

'Blood grievances are for disputes between common men and knights,' he boomed in exasperation. 'Not to be pursued against magistrates, barons and Seidhr! If you learn anything from your brother's death, let it be that!'

Jhonan let the sword fall from his hand, discarding it like an unwanted obligation. The resound of steel on stone was met with silence between the Vornirs. Their unspoken thoughts were rewarded with hisses and crackles from the fireplace, sounds reminiscent of the funeral pyre.

The feelings struggling in Daimonia's heart chose this moment to reach full bloom and she wept. She fell helplessly into her grandfather's steadying arms, the fight draining from her. His fear of the Accord was becoming her own, dowsing the fire she had felt so strongly. She was succumbing to his sense of futility.

Jhonan held her tightly. 'My anger could fill the sea, but I won't lose you, Daimonia. Oh Goddess, no. Not you, my dear girl.'

She pulled away from him, repulsed by his unwelcome sentiments. 'Then I will go to my mother! Surely the great Captain Catherine will not let her son die unavenged! If she had been here, none of this would have happened!'

'No, Dai. That road will only lead to more sorrow. Catherine may be a famous knight, but she cannot love you as I do.'

'You? A fingerless fool? A ruin of a man incapable of caring for a gentle boy! A creature proud to be violent and drunk! You cannot love me better than my own mother.'

Jhonan stared at the unquenchable fury with a look of horrified recognition.

'It was you who drove Niklos into that life.' Daimonia aimed her words like arrows. 'He was no warrior, but you filled him with the idea of it. *Men fight*, that's what you told him!' She seemed to grow taller in the shadows, to leer over the old man, dominating him. 'Do not stand against me or I will add your blood to the chalice.'

Jhonan fell to his knees, his spirit failing. 'Then I see I have truly become your father.'

ACT TWO

THE WAY KNIGHT

The Way Knight

The booming voice of a travelling merchant woke all of Jaromir. Dalibor's itinerant traders had developed a sales dialect that involved slurring a whole cluster of words into one. The result was a rambling monologue, where the names of goods could be occasionally identified amid what sounded like coarse language.

Daimonia set out from Vornir Manor wearing her favourite boots, a riding cloak and a long black dress with a scalloped lace neckline. Her raven hair flowed over her shoulders and back. A few heads turned as she passed by. The adventurous girl who had once climbed trees and played in the woods was fast becoming a woman.

The girl was oblivious to all attention but her own; with blue eyes beneath black brows, she was fixed on her own purpose. The cold morning made her feel vitalised and sharp. She had nothing in common with the old fool she had left behind, sleeping drunkenly in his chair. She had stolen his Visoth war dagger and wore it sheathed on her belt.

Alongside her she led the horse taken from the road watchman. It was a disconcertingly large beast laden with the watchman's leather saddle and sword, a satchel of clothes, food and Daimonia's bow.

'Daimonia!' Lurching through the crowd came Villiam the Fool. He paid no mind to those he bumped and jostled as he ran. The youth was taller and broader than anyone in the village and his wild tangled hair had never been cut. He held a whole loaf of bread in one hand and a thickness of wood in the other. 'Are we going now?' he asked Daimonia. 'We go together.'

'No, Villiam.' She smiled. 'I'm sorry. This is not your journey.'

'I'm your brother now,' he reminded her of his promise at the funeral.

There was no being unkind to Villiam, he simply had no understanding. 'It's my mother I need now,' she told him and tried to escape. Her eyes were on the small market and she strode up to stand behind the gathering crowd.

'There is not enough love for the living, let alone the dead!' Villiam shouted after her.

Daimonia knew where he had got that from; it was a line from the play. The boy was a talented mimic and sounded just like the actor, but didn't understand what came out of his own mouth. She refused to turn around, focusing instead on what she needed.

The merchant was a short man with a canny look about him. He was employing a base eloquence to gather a growing crowd of villagers to his stall. On display was a selection of glass, fabrics and jewellery, which the merchant had no doubt procured at lower prices from Leechfinger. The success of his enterprise was well evidenced by the generous fatness of his son, who was busy laying out the goods.

Knowing that no merchant would chance the trade route without protection, Daimonia looked keenly for some Way Knights. Daimonia allowed her imagination to play with the idea of travelling with a pair of handsome warriors and becoming a little infatuated with one or both of them. A premonition of warmth exuded from the romance of her imaginations.

Beyond the crowd, a solitary Way Knight tended to his horse. There was a weighty surety to his movements that made him easy to watch. He was clad in tarnished chain armour and a magnificent plate helm. His fraying blood-coloured tabard was blazoned with the symbol of a wheel with swords for spokes. The same symbol was painted on a battle-dented shield discarded by his feet.

'Good morning, sir.' Daimonia tried to sound precise like her mother. 'I would like to enlist your services.'

The Way Knight froze at the sound of the girl's voice, his armoured shoulders rising in apprehension. After an uncomfortable moment he reluctantly turned to give Daimonia a wary stare. His eyes were half closed with mistrust, his face a dense map of old gashes and deep lacerations. Scar upon scar travelled across his features, giving his flesh the appearance of a weathered pathway.

Daimonia tried to tame her expression as she felt her mouth turn in disgust. An inadvertent noise escaped her lips and she blinked repeatedly. Struggling to manage her feelings, she looked squarely at the knight as if the task was not repugnant.

The knight advanced towards her, his appearance improving not one bit with proximity. Daimonia found herself scrutinising anything other than the ruined features. She feigned interest in his armour and his strong thick hands. Inevitably she met his cold gaze and found herself speculating on the cause of the prolific scarring; those injuries were something more sinister than a knight's war wounds.

'I'm Goodkin,' he growled an introduction. His lips were as cracked and dry as his voice.

Daimonia considered running at that moment. How could she spend days in the company of this monster?

'I hoped to travel with you as far as Khorgov,' Daimonia felt obliged to explain.

'Not a good time.' He breathed heavily as if speech was an exertion. 'There have been Baoth raids along the coast.'

'Yes, I hear the invaders like Dallish women,' Daimonia joked.

Goodkin stared at her as if at an idiot. 'The Baoth only kill the men, this is true. You would be taken back to their homeland as a slave and enjoy less rights than an animal.'

'I didn't mean—'

'You would be made to worship the Burning Man,' the monstrous knight continued. 'Forced to observe all the rites of their faith. In time you would come to fear Gorach Baoth and think us Goddess worshippers merely savages.' He raised his fist. 'You would love the hand that strikes you.'

Foreign raids were a good excuse not to travel with the disfigured man, but there was an inferred challenge in the Way Knight's warning, something that provoked Daimonia to resolution.

'I have the coin for my journey,' Daimonia told him firmly. She offered a silver piece, remembering the old rhyme.

Fare well on your journey
She who pays the Way Knight's fee
For an offering of silver denarii
He will lay down his life for thee

Goodkin took the denarius as if condemned by it. Impressed on its surface was a portrait of the prince.

They left Jaromir later that day. The group travelling under the Way Knight's protection consisted of Daimonia Vornir, the travelling merchant Purtur and his large son Hem. Both Purtur and his boy drove horse-drawn carts brimming with goods.

'Thank the Great Mother we got Sir Goodkin,' Purtur confided in Daimonia. 'Any outlaws will be frightened off by one glance at his face!'

Daimonia glanced uneasily at the Way Knight, who insisted on riding behind the others. He looked every bit the threat travellers hoped to avoid. 'All those scars, are they wounds of war?'

'War? No!' Purtur snorted. 'Such extremities must've been inflicted by a woman! A jealous wife, I've no doubt. Or even better, his mother!'

'A mother loves her own child.' Daimonia waved away Purtur's speculations.

'That why you're travelling all the way to Khorgov to see yours? Hah!

You're Catherine Vornir's daughter, you claim? All very well, but I bet you haven't seen her for years.'

Daimonia's face filled with black anger. But Purtur was right. It had been long years.

'Shouldn't show your feelings like that,' Purtur continued, giving out his free wisdom. 'You're pretty in an odd kind of way when you're not scowling. Certainly the fairest face I saw in Jaromir anyway. Hah! You'll have no trouble finding a husband. In fact, my son Hem isn't married yet!'

Daimonia glanced back at Purtur's son. 'That's because he looks like a potato.'

Jaromir lay in a shallow basin surrounded by a vast plentiful forest. Once the travellers had escaped to higher ground, they could glimpse the coast and wonder at the barbaric lands beyond the grey waves. Daimonia's imagination sailed with tales of their ancient rivals the Visoth, a warlike folk who called the stars heroes and rode in wooden serpents. Now those former foes traded with the Dallish and shared a mutual enemy in the inhuman Baoth.

By late afternoon they could see a military garrison in the distance. The fortified structure was surrounded by plummeting valleys on three sides. A further earthen rampart stretched along the coast for miles. Even from so far away, the reassuring sight eased fears about invaders. Daimonia mused that such securities came at a high price. She let an old drinking song of Jhonan's drift from her lips.

Don't send your son to the army, sir,
Don't send your son to the army.
For the dead don't drink
And their corpses stink,
Don't send your son to the army.

A reeking smoke rolled across the coast as daylight waned and the brilliant stars awakened. A cold silence fell among the travellers as they made camp along the edge of the forest. Goodkin allowed them no fire.

'Smell that?' Purtur whispered to Daimonia and Hem. 'That burning in your throat is the smell of cooked children roasted by Baoth cannibals.' He watched their anxious faces with undisguised glee. 'Behind the war masks of the Baoth are the faces of animals! Creatures who torture themselves till they reach a war-madness, spurring them to acts of strange violence!'

The Way Knight was standing away from the others. He was an armoured silhouette holding a chained coin reverently between his fingers.

'Is Sir Goodkin a Baoth?' Hem whispered fearfully. 'He has the face of a beast and he fights like one too!'

'Silence,' Goodkin ordered and the chattering immediately ceased. He turned to the girl, his helm shrouding his grisly face with shadow. 'Here are the Way Knights' rules of travel, and if you stray from them, you may die.' He paused and drew up several hungry breaths before his throaty voice continued. 'First, you stay always with me. Second, you provoke no enemy. Third, you commit no crime nor trespass against the

Accord.'

Daimonia let go a little giggle at the Way Knight's intensity. *Does he think me a fool?* 'You don't need to worry about me.' She brushed away his concerns.

Goodkin's shoulders rose with heavy breaths. 'Ask me how many girls I've seen die.'

'I'm sorry.' Daimonia blushed. 'I'll follow your rules.'

'Ask me!' Goodkin insisted.

'I said I'd obey. You have my promise on it,' Daimonia vowed.

A Visitor

Once everyone was snoring, Hem decided it was safe to move. He slowly sat up, careful not to wake the others, and cautiously tiptoed through the camp. Hem's father, Purtur, slept with a stumpy wooden club held against his chest, as if that would serve to bat away the Baoth horde. Way Knight Goodkin reclined against a solid oak, his face clad in darkness and one hand clenching his hefty sword. Hem wondered how many men the weapon had sped to the Great Mother. He decided to give the sleeping knight a wide berth.

Hem found Daimonia on the edge of the camp, crowned by leaves as she slept beneath the glittering Eye. She was nothing like the girls his mother wanted him to marry. For one thing she was the most serious girl Hem had ever seen, her dark brows always low with intense thought or raised high in question. Hem imagined she felt things very deeply. Who knew what dreams embraced her?

Hem had watched Daimonia all day, seen her riding on her great horse like a queen. He was sure she had smiled at him once or twice.

Had a feeling passed between them? Love was painful and confusing, like a wonderful ache.

Sadly, Daimonia was the only good thing that had come out of Jaromir. Something Hem had eaten had upset his stomach horribly and he needed to shit desperately. It was bad enough doing it out in the open. The Purtur family house had its own toilet and Hem was used to privacy. But to have to do it anywhere near Daimonia was just too embarrassing. So Hem wandered on until he was a safe distance away from the camp. He untied his baggy leggings and squatted behind a tree, hoping no bugs crawled up his arse.

The release was sudden and noisy. Hem recoiled at the stench, cursing lest it was so potent as to reach the others.

A primal guttural sound cut the night. Hem froze, his guts churning with fear. Stuck mid-dropping, he wriggled, trying to finish what he had started. There was an awful voice and abruptly a pale corpse ran jerkily into the clearing.

Hem shrieked at the wrinkly thing. It was drawn forward by a bloated phallus, as if the rest of its saggy body were merely an appendage to its lust.

Too indisposed to run, Hem began scrabbling for some leaves to clean himself, his fingers clutching desperately at mud and twigs. He fell onto his side, half into his own mess, and cried. All his strength seemed to have vanished; his hands were trembling uncontrollably.

The shape was upon him. It pressed Hem to the earth and began to convulse over the boy, who sobbed in confusion and despair.

A shout announced the hasty arrival of Sir Goodkin followed by

Purtur, both charging into the clearing. Inexplicably they stopped and instead of helping simply stared confused at Hem, who lay paralysed in a mess of shit and leaves.

'Get up, you disgusting boy!' Purtur demanded. 'Are you a complete fool? Rolling in your own waste and shrieking?'

'But, Father.' Hem sobbed. He twisted about, staring into the trees, but there was nothing.

'You will get us all killed,' Goodkin rebuked the boy furiously, his eyes watering with anger.

Hem saw the thing again the following day, but under even stranger circumstances. They had set off early at Goodkin's insistence, and Hem had been trying not to look at Daimonia. He felt unclean after the previous night's horror and was afraid he might somehow spread some of that nastiness onto the girl if he stared at her too much.

'Rest your backside from that great horse.' Purtur had coaxed Daimonia down from her impressive mount. 'Ride on Hem's wagon. He's never spoken with a real lady before!'

Hem felt his face redden so hotly that it must have seemed obvious to everyone that he loved her. Riding through the overcast morning, Hem fixated on the way ahead, not daring to look at the girl more than once every mile. She was extremely fidgety and would yawn and stretch, sigh occasionally and even sing.

Her voice wasn't like that of the girls back home at Littlecrook. Those voices were full of hay from the fields, rolling hills and summer mornings. Daimonia's voice was not like that at all. When she sang it was like the last voice at the end of time.

When the guiding light has gone,
And has left me all alone,
Will you still ride by my side?
Who will be there to take me home?

'What's that from?' Hem stammered.

'What?'

'That song. I've never heard it before.'

'It's from a play.'

'I'm not sure what you mean.'

'The travelling players. Haven't you seen them? They travel performing the myth of the Goddess.'

'No.'

'Well, you should see it for yourself.'

Hem wrestled with conflicting feelings. He had managed the brief exchange quite ably, but couldn't help but notice Daimonia's dismissive tone. He felt a tiny pain well up inside. The cart continued jolting along while Hem mustered himself for a second go at conversation.

'What's it about? The song?'

This time Daimonia looked right at Hem, as if weighing the authenticity of his interest.

'The Goddess has lost everyone she loved,' she told him finally. 'But one day she will see them again. They will all be held by the Great Mother.'

'I think it's a bit confusing.' Hem stroked at his furry chin. 'Aren't the

Goddess and Great Mother Cerenox the same person? And then there's curious Ceresoph and dreadful Cere-Thalatte!'

'Is the child the same as the youth, or the youth the same as the adult?'

'Yes.' Hem shook the reins. 'Well, yes and no, because if I met myself as a child, then I'm not sure how much we'd have in common. You know, playing with snails and the like. But if I were an old man…'

'Sounds like you've understood it very well.'

Hem blushed. 'We're not all stupid in Littlecrook, you know. My ma reads us stories 'n everything.'

Hem waited for an acknowledgement but Daimonia said nothing. She stared at the path ahead as if hurrying the journey along. Sometimes she would watch the Way Knight riding ahead, whose formidable form reminded Hem of his own insufficiencies.

'I expect you can read.' Hem broke the silence.

'Yes.'

'I thought so.' Hem blinked happily. 'My ma always said I should marry a clever girl.'

There was a yell up ahead and Daimonia leaped from the cart.

Feeling that the rug had been pulled from under him, Hem slowed the horse and watched the girl running off. 'It wasn't a proposal or anything,' he called uselessly into the wind.

Dismounting, Hem strolled towards Daimonia and the Way Knight. They were speaking with a finely dressed man wearing a feathered felt hat worn atop an extravagant golden wig.

'I realise this is a terrible inconvenience.' The man was twisting his blond curls as he spoke. 'But I was robbed blind, and if I could just join you as far as Knave, I would be greatly obliged.'

Hem winced to see Goodkin pull off his helm and wipe his scarred brow. From here the Way Knight could not see Hem staring at the festival of wounds across his head. But nevertheless it felt safer not to look too long.

'Pay the Way Knight's fee,' Goodkin told the traveller. 'I'll see you safely to Knave.'

'You do remember the part about me getting robbed?' The traveller went to put a friendly hand on Goodkin's shoulder, but the Way Knight brushed it away. 'You can't mean to leave me here for the sake of a single denarius!'

'I will pay his fee,' Daimonia offered.

'That's what I was about to say.' Hem caught up with them, breathless. He bent over gasping after the short run. 'I was just going to offer to pay it. Can't leave him here on the road to get robbed again!'

The Way Knight turned to Hem and held out his palm. Hem was confused for a moment, looking to Daimonia, who had offered first. Then with the least reluctant face he could manage, he gave Goodkin a denarius.

From the other cart Purtur let out a loud unimpressed rasp.

The traveller removed his hat and fanned his face. Beneath the glamour of his curly wig, his skin was saggy with age and his eyes bloodshot. 'Most kind of you,' he thanked Hem with an appreciative, albeit limp handshake.

Hem tilted his head curiously, sensing that he'd seen the fellow before. He had barely taken a step back towards the cart when it dawned on him. He froze, recalling the previous night's horror and the thing thrusting lustily at him. Surely he was mistaken; that thing had been practically a corpse. He turned and gaped over his shoulder to see the wrinkled wigged thing smiling at him hideously.

'What is that smell?' Daimonia asked when the carts had set off again.

'Horses,' Hem whimpered. His bowels had let him down and a wet patch of pee now reeked from his trousers. *I'm a damp wet idiot! A damp wet idiot!* He let it circle around his mind until he was hitting himself in the face to the beat of it.

'What are you doing?' Daimonia yelled. She wrestled with Hem, trying to stop him. Hem tried to push her off and her palm accidentally sank into his soaking crotch.

Daimonia pulled away quickly, smelling her hand in revulsion and then wiping it roughly on his jacket. 'You're disgusting!' She leapt off and ran to Purtur's cart.

Hem watched her go and glared at the wigged thing that was making friendly conversation with his father. He wanted to shout and scream with all his might, but instead his anger curled and twisted and turned against him.

The Fate of Jhonan Vornir

Kraljevic was alive with celebration, every street and balcony filled with feverish excitement. Adjurators and holy celebrants led a great procession of youths dancing through the crowd, parading the regal colours, silver and red. The capital city had never seen so auspicious an event; a great revelation was at hand.

Through the streets a beautiful white-veiled bride roamed. The woman was heavy with child and groaning with the pain preceding birth. She staggered bloody-footed through the streets, sometimes falling to one knee as the jubilant peasants righted her and sent her on her way with a cheer. While all others rejoiced, she alone was in distress.

'Where are you?' she cried, searching everywhere for her bridegroom. She fell again, bloodying the knee of her white dress.

A number of false suitors presented themselves, filling the air with their boasting. The bride turned from each one, growing ever more desperate as they pulled at her. Only she would know the true bridegroom.

Beyond a canal bridge a golden man stood watching silently. He made no boasts nor did he dance like the intoxicated fools. He simply waited for the bride to come. His face was stuck in a never-ending scream.

The Geld Knight Conrad Ernst awoke abruptly with a frightened whimper. He tried to sit and immediately seethed at the soreness of his wounds. Naked beneath the glaring stars, he carefully examined every part of his body. His hands probed tentatively around the various injuries inflicted by Jhonan Vornir.

The pit of his arm was a clumsily stitched mess, evidence that Fotter's medical skills had been grotesquely exaggerated. Conrad's fingers crept fearfully towards the bulbous mess that had been his testicles. They were fat with discoloured bruising and the texture was both damp and scabby. He tentatively tried to stoke his desire, but the pain was excruciating. He quickly withdrew his hand, an involuntary tremble emasculating him further.

'Vornir bastard!' he cursed.

The Geld Knight was camped in the forest beyond Jaromir, his mind chewing incessantly on a feast of self-pity and vindictive urges. He preferred to establish his own space a distance from his Geld enforcers, who were essentially poor and greedy criminals capable of anything. Some of the girls from the village had been foolish enough to follow these under-men out into the woods. Their screams and whines had now subsided into the groans of the forest.

Conrad considered sending as many as four men to slay Vornir, but he had the apprehension that none would return alive. He began to fastidiously brush and rebrush his hair while reflecting on strategies and general principles of revenge. A pleasant recollection uncoiled from the many branches of his memory.

After the High Adjurator had met with a hideous accident, Conrad's potential had been recognised by an influential statesman and advisor to the prince. Advisor Pavel had been writing a justification of the atrocities of war and young Conrad was selected as his scribe.

They had laboured together in the austere chambers of the royal library, a place troubled by eerie Archonian relics indecipherable to scholars. Here Conrad and his new mentor had worked to make history more palatable through the artifice of words.

'Why did Prince Moranion not lay siege to Lord Erleth's castle after Erleth betrayed him?' Conrad had asked Advisor Pavel.

'Often an enemy will invite attack where they are strongest,' Pavel had observed. 'A knight seeks justification in a contest of arms. A scholar prefers a battle of wits, while a woman's weapons are gossip and slander.'

'Lord Erleth's castle is said to be impregnable,' Conrad acknowledged.

'Unlike his wife,' Pavel quipped. 'Which was why Prince Moranion broke Erleth, not with a siege weapon but with his cock!'

'But what of honour, master? Did not the prince diminish himself further by repaying Erleth's error of character with adultery?'

'What is honour?' Pavel was fond of perplexing questions. He would appear at times to know nothing about the most obvious facts, only to then expose some nuance or fallacy.

Conrad relished these little challenges. 'It seems to me that honour is the way a man conducts himself so as to warrant the esteem of others.'

Pavel rewarded Conrad with a thin smile. 'Honour is a noise, a sound. An utterance designed to connote a set of ideas. Who decides what is honourable?'

'I suppose we do, master. We who write these histories.'

'This is why I have chosen you,' Pavel acknowledged. 'You do not blush at the duplicity required of great men.'

'I see that no man is great who cannot convince another of it.'

'You grin like a girl, far too pleased with yourself. Do you think that is an original thought, boy?'

'It is original to me,' young Conrad had defended.

'Understand this,' Pavel asserted. 'If your enemy be possessed of strong arguments, destroy his reputation. If he be not corruptible, have him slain in a duel. If he be a great warrior, have him die in his sleep.'

Conrad ceased his combing and allowed himself a private smile. He called into the forest, summoning the young enforcer Scorcher, who the magistrates claimed had a talent for this kind of task. Together they shared a drink and then the boy was sent to work.

Stroking his swollen testicles, Conrad watch Jaromir become gradually illuminated by a rising pillar of fire. The flames climbed and arched into the sky, lifting like a hot sword to challenge the very stars. The old watchtower made a magnificent furnace, more glorious than the Eye of Ceresoph.

Conrad watched long enough to be certain the old bastard and his precious granddaughter would have been cooked alive. He imagined he heard their screams rolling on the wind, smouldering husks of flesh crying out to their silent Goddess.

Conrad's face was aglow with the victory, basking in the light of his superiority. He heard the voice of the Secret God whispering *you are the one!*

The Dispossessed

'So you're Catherine Vornir's daughter?' the traveller asked, tipping his hat graciously. His voice was rich, but his beautiful wig was infested with bugs, forcing Daimonia to lean away from him in the cart. The traveller had been speaking effusively about famous places and people whilst frequently touching Daimonia's knee to punctuate his exclamations. Each time his elderly hand came near her leg, she would duck to avoid his writhing wig.

'Purtur was just telling me you've a famous mother,' the traveller enthused. 'You know, the Vornirs had a fierce reputation when I was a boy. Cross a Vornir and you'd be looking over your shoulder forever!' Beneath all his finery, the traveller was so extraordinarily wrinkly that when he frowned, his whole face seemed to sag.

He had introduced himself as Svek, a courier for the Seidhr and responsible for transporting documents, writs, occasionally even children on their behalf.

'Do you know my mother personally?' Daimonia asked cautiously. She was forced to dodge the wig again as the traveller leaned close to answer her question.

'I've heard of her fine work fighting rebels.' Svek nodded vigorously. 'I hear Captain Vornir is a favourite of the prince. He adores great women!'

Daimonia suppressed a smile as she mapped her ambitions. She would find her mother and together they would mourn Niklos' death, taking comfort in each other's arms. When the time of tears was done, they would ride together to Kraljevic and bring their case before Prince Moranion. Sharing their anger as if it were his own, the prince would have the baron investigated. Volk Leechfinger would have to fight in the Meat Pit, to be scorned by everyone and slaughtered. Or better still, he would be banished to dread Archonia.

Daimonia could picture the baron as surely as if he were standing before her: his entitled gestures, his curling lashes and lusty smile. He was a man she would destroy in her brother's name.

Niklos, she prayed, *the Accord will yet yield justice on your behalf.*

'Miss Vornir?' Svek was asking.

'I'm sorry, what were you saying?'

'I said is it your plan to follow in your mother's footsteps? Leading men into battle, and rooting out traitors and spies?'

I'm going to root someone out, Daimonia promised.

A lopsided statue loomed amid clumps of moss, marking the territory of Garst. The sinking stone depicted a bald figure with a maleficent expression, gesticulating towards the stars. Birds had decorated the bald head with their offerings and some of the extremities were snapped off.

'Who is that dreadful figure?' Daimonia enquired.

'Dreadful?' Svek raised his eyebrows. 'That is the likeness of Adjurator Garst, a great benefactor to the people of the southern shires.

The village ahead took its esteemed name from his own.'

'He's long dead now, I assume.'

'I would assume so.' Svek nodded. 'His career was ruined by malicious rumours and he had to retire from public life. His many kindnesses were forgotten because of the lies of boys!'

'More likely he thought he was above the Accord,' Purtur sneered. 'People like that think they are better than the rest of us!'

Grave-grey smoke clogged the air as the day waned. A flock of refugee birds followed the coast, seeking fresher climes. The Eye of Ceresoph began to open.

The travellers continued on, keen to make Garst village before night descended. The horses pulled through boggy mud, enduring mosquitos and gnats. Here the forest was gnarled and full of natural trenches. Conversations waned and a weary silence fell over the group.

At the tail of a muddy track, a huge weathered tree loomed like a veined hand exploding from the earth. Pairs of blood-clotted shackles were nailed to the scarred and bloodstained bark. A tangible sensation of suffering lingered around the tortured wood.

'Some terrible crime was done here.' Daimonia's breath became short and she found herself clinging to the wagon as if to prevent falling.

'More accurate to say a crime was redressed,' Svek corrected. 'Is there no hurting post in Jaromir? No place for answering minor infractions of the Accord?'

'Answering them with what?'

'Well, it depends.' Svek curled his golden wig in his bony fingers. 'A troublesome neighbour might be restrained here and pelted with rotten fruit. More grievous offences could incur beatings or even lashings.'

'I don't like it,' Daimonia decided. A shiver crept along her shoulders.

'Neither do I,' Hem added timorously. He drew his cart alongside Purtur's and seemed highly agitated. Daimonia's horse was tethered to Hem's cart and tried to pull away as they stopped.

'You'd be glad of it,' Purtur butted in, 'if you lived in as miserable an arse-pit as Garst! You ain't never met a more suspicious people, distrusting their own neighbours and bolting their doors at night!'

'You're not filling me with confidence,' Svek moaned. 'I was hoping to draw some funds from the local scir and have neither seal nor papers left to establish my authority.'

'Well, I ain't calling 'em backwards or anything,' Purtur explained. 'But this one time a fellow came here to build a kiln. The locals thought it was a shrine to Gorach Baoth and they roasted him to death!'

Beyond the hurting post a sooty wind writhed and danced. As they pressed forward, the travellers wept and coughed, choking on the saturating smog. They emerged from the trail to meet a scene of ashen gloom.

The village had been eradicated, pulled apart like the toy of a malicious infant. Frames and rafters were splayed like broken fingers. Joints of human flesh lay chewed in the grass. Clusters of shambling figures haunted the dereliction.

'Baoth have been here,' Goodkin snarled. 'Could be here still. We'll find another way.'

'Nonsense!' Purtur frowned defiantly. 'You know what I smell?'

'Smoke?' Daimonia coughed.

'Opportunity!' Purtur cackled. 'These people have lost everything and I'm in a position to sell it back to them!' He rode his cart directly into the village, flashing his tongue at the knight.

'Bloody fool!' Svek shouted, trying to climb over Purtur to get out. 'Go back!'

A skulking shape leapt from the shadows, hands touching ankles like an ape. Tendrils swung from its head, flapping as it moved. It let out a hiss as it leapt onto Purtur's cart and landed on Daimonia.

Daimonia pushed her hands into the creature's wet face. Beyond its savage eyes, Daimonia could see that it was a man clothed in the hair and skin of other men. Its teeth were like nails, its breath venomous.

'Get it off!' she squealed.

The Baoth raised a weapon hewn from bone, then dropped it again as Goodkin galloped past, hewing its head with his broadsword. The neck vomited profusely.

Daimonia screamed and shoved the carcass off. More shapes were emerging from the smoke, brandishing spines and skulls, hooked blades and tusk-white scimitars. They were everywhere, like a colony of ants swarming from the ground.

'Ride!' Goodkin roared, racing ahead of the cart and turning his horse around. Dusty figures leapt at his mount, fastening themselves to the horse with sinuous arms and hungry teeth. The animal collapsed and Goodkin vanished into the dust.

'Chrestos save us!' Purtur wailed, steering the cart around. He was shaking as if wracked by lightning, his nose streaming with runny mucus.

Daimonia turned to see the Way Knight silhouetted in the smog. He fought like a series of pictures in a book; his sword raised high in the air, then plunging to split flesh, every flash of movement alive with muscular force.

'We can't leave Goodkin behind!'

'What are you talking about?' Purtur shouted. 'He's paid to protect us!'

Hem was ahead of them, rushing his carriage into the shadowed pockets of woodland ahead.

Daimonia trembled with fear and anger. She longed to be there with Goodkin, fighting the Baoth horde even to her own death. But she could barely move her fingers and the cart was cascading away from the clamour and violence.

From the cover of bushes a figure ran out, waving desperately to hail the speeding carts. 'Please!' The man shouted, 'Stop!' A whole family began to emerge from the thicket, crawling from their hiding place.

'I beg you,' the young father called to Hem. 'Can you spare a little food? And if you've room, please take us with you!'

Daimonia watched Hem's concerned expression as the boy slowed his cart to survey the family. The man's wife was a fair-haired Visoth, snuggling her newborn baby to her breast. Two young children raced around impatiently, competing to get close to the horses.

'Father, we must help them!' Hem hollered from his cart.

'You've a generous heart, son,' Purtur called back as he pulled up alongside. 'But there's always greedy fingers looking for a free handout. I call them lazy who can't make their own prosperity.'

'But the Baoth took everything,' Hem pleaded. 'They didn't ask for that!'

'Are you going to help all the poor of Dalibor?' Purtur challenged bitterly. 'Are you going to give to everyone who asks until you have nothing left yourself?'

'I don't know.'

'Stupid boy!' Purtur spat in the air, his face raspberry red. 'What would you be if we gave everything away?'

'I wouldn't be fat.'

'As an affiliate of the Seidhr, I cannot see this family go without support!' Svek stood and whipped off his hat. He smiled at the children, coils of skin ringing his lips. 'We simply must assist them, Purtur.'

'You didn't even have the coin for your own journey,' Purtur reminded the courier.

'They can ride with me,' Hem determined.

'We have coin.' The young father weighed a pouch of silver. 'What we need is a safe place for our children. If you can take us as far as Chalkwater, we have family there who can help.'

Goodkin rode into the clearing, eyes dark beneath his visor. His armour was slick with blood; his horse scratched and slashed, its beautiful mane torn out.

'Get into the carts,' he told the family breathlessly.

'They ain't climbing all over my cart.' Purtur had the look of a disgruntled boy.

The Way Knight rounded on the merchant, his voice brimming with murderous rage. 'Yes, they are!' he bellowed. He dismounted and began hefting the children up.

'Much obliged.' The father grinned as if he had already arrived in Chalkwater and was enjoying a bottle of ale. 'I'm Fletcher,' he told them. 'This is my wife, Isolde.' He took the baby as she climbed onto the cart. 'Is anyone alive back there?'

Goodkin brushed debris from his tabard. 'No,' he replied.

Masks of the Seidhr

Daimonia awoke to a child's hands on her cheeks. Big blue eyes stared into her own as the girl laughed at Daimonia's surprised expression.

'Wakey,' the girl said, patting Daimonia's forehead with a fat palm.

'Hello, little one.' Daimonia grinned. She rubbed her eyes and sat up from her crunchy bed of leaves. A gorgeous dawn lit the forest, lifting her heart with renewing radiance. The chubby child took Daimonia's arm, encouraging her to rise.

Daimonia stood, rising to her tiptoes as she stretched and shook loose her fatigue. Her nightmares had been stranger than ever: grandfather Jhonan transformed into a sad old tree that no one loved. The dream had filled her with a melancholy that the morning made ridiculous with its truth-giving light.

'Pray,' the child instructed. She held her hands up to the sky as her wispy hair tickled her forehead and nose.

Daimonia sang the morning prayer alongside the girl's stumbling recitation. Swords of dust cut through the high branches to illuminate their faces.

Chrestos, be my brother
When the morning light ascends.
Be my shield, my torch, my armour
Guard until my journey ends.

When I've wandered into darkness
Lost within the perilous night
Will you follow me, my brother?
Brother Chrestos, join my fight.

'You're crying.' The child was concerned. She imitated a sad face, scrunching her hands into fists and rubbing her round cheeks.

'I'm not,' Daimonia assured her. 'I'm just tired.'

'Who is Chrestos?' the infant wondered.

'He's the brother and friend of the Goddess.'

'Like my brother Bran?'

'Yes.' Daimonia lifted the girl up. 'Just like Bran.'

'Have you got a brother?' the child questioned, running her little fingers through Daimonia's leafy hair.

'We'd better find your family.' Daimonia lowered her tone. 'Everyone will be wondering where you've gone.'

Returning to the group, Daimonia was met with a singular sight. The forest was full of strange gleaming faces; silver-masked women in fine purple robes glided around the camp, questioning everyone. Daimonia's first instinct was to hide, quickly slipping behind a tree.

'Who are those women?' Daimonia asked the girl.

'Pickle.'

'What?'

'Pickle!' the girl shouted insistently. She poked her thumb towards herself.

'Hush!' Daimonia raised a finger to her lips. 'Who are those ladies, Pickle?'

'Cider,' the child attempted.

'Seidhr?' Daimonia's eyes widened as she peered around the tree. So these were women of the Seidhr Order, she realised, staring at the tall figures. They moved with imperious grace and asserted themselves with complete confidence. Around each waist was a leather belt containing small satchels, an ornate seal of office and a sheathed blade.

Daimonia found Hem on the fringe of the group. 'What's going on?' she asked.

'Seidhr workers,' he told her anxiously. 'They've just inspected the Fletcher children, but I don't think they'll take them away.'

'Why would they take them away?'

'Well, in case they're in danger and all that.' Hem stumbled over his explanation. 'I don't know if the children are all that safe with us, to be honest. I'm a bit worried about–'

'Take them where?'

'I don't know. To the baron, I suppose. But listen, about Svek–'

She was already walking away, leaving Hem gaping mid-sentence.

There were four women in the clearing, along with their horses, a cage-carriage and the brawniest Accord Knight Daimonia had ever seen. The women were in discussion with Svek, who seemed to be quite in his element discoursing with the workers.

'I doubt you'll find any orphans in Garst,' he was telling them with an amiable smile. 'The whole place has been reduced to a Baoth cesspit.' He pulled at the folds of skin beneath his chin. 'As for the Fletcher family, I'll see that the little ones get to Chalkwater safely. You can rely on me. I've plenty of experience with children.'

'What happens to the children?' Daimonia demanded. She walked up to confront the tallest Seidhr worker and stood close enough to see her own reflection in the silver mask.

'Who is this youth?' the woman asked with the merest tip of her head. Her mask was designed to pretend the most benevolent and beautiful face imaginable.

'I'm Daimonia Vornir.'

'Vornir?' Behind her ornate mask the Seidhr's eyes narrowed. 'Sisters, isn't Vornir one of the names in the Book of Traitors?'

Daimonia felt her face redden, though whether from fear or anger it was hard to say.

'*Catherine* Vornir holds a captaincy in the Accord and is, I believe, the castellan of Khorgov Fortress,' Svek informed them respectfully. 'If the name is familiar, might I suggest it is because this is the famous lady's daughter.'

'I see.' Eyes relaxed behind the mask. 'Well, Miss Vornir, I can assure you each child we gather will be fed and looked after. Our work is the most important in all of Dalibor, although we are rarely thanked for it.'

'Why do you have that huge warrior with you?' Daimonia pointed to the Accord Knight, who was supping greedily from his wineskin. 'In case the children don't want to leave?'

'You're being facetious. No one travels the coast without–'

'And who decides where the children go?'

'A council of senior authorities–'

'You mean the baron!' Daimonia's thumb caressed the dagger at her belt.

A firm hand gripped Daimonia's arm and dragged her away. The terrible face of the Way Knight leaned in closely. For the first time she became intimate with the savagery of his facial wounds. She morbidly imagined tracing a finger through the valleys of his flesh.

'Remember the rules of travel,' he murmured, squeezing her arm sharply. 'Provoke no enemy, nor do any trespass against the Accord.'

'And stay with you. Yes, I remember!' she complained, pulling herself away.

'Well, I think we are done here,' the senior Seidhr announced. 'There are families desperate for our intervention.' She shot a sharp look at Daimonia before leading her group away.

'Mount up,' Goodkin told everyone. 'Enough time wasted.'

Along the forest trail the carts rumbled, venturing through wooded tunnels of green and gold. All day Goodkin chose to ride out in front, patiently leading the procession as day became night.

Daimonia was caught by the treasury of light above. The Eye of Ceresoph was bright tonight, twinkling with mischievous radiance. Daimonia fancied she could hear its roaring intensity. The gleaming Eye was the point through which the curious Goddess had gazed into the universe and inadvertently created all life. Her seeds, the stars, were cast into every heart and within them a longing to return to her bosom.

'Best not let you take the reins,' Purtur teased. 'Or we'll crash into those stars.'

'They're our brothers and sisters, our missing fathers.'

'You believe all that stuff?' Purtur weighed the girl with his stare.

'I believe the Goddess promised to free us from this world one day.'

'I hope that day doesn't come soon.' Purtur winced. 'I've money to make!'

'Money!' Daimonia chided. 'What is money anyway?'

'What do you mean – what is it? Everyone knows what money is! And everyone wants it!'

'Imagine I'd never heard of it and then explain to me what it is.'

Purtur shook his head as if indulging a simpleton. 'It's something that the more of it you have, the happier you are.'

'Is that really the relationship between money and happiness?'

'Of course!' Purtur chortled. 'Why else would I be risking my life, even risking my son's life, to travel around making more of it?'

Lights appeared along the forest path. A caravan was approaching from the east. The foremost carriage was illuminated by the homely radiance of a glass lantern giving glow to the fashioned wood.

As the strangers drew near, Daimonia observed their harried faces. They were looking ruefully at Goodkin and seemed disturbed and afraid.

'Turn back,' an old driver warned. On his lap he cradled a young man whose tunic was sopping with blood. The boy clutched at something in one crimson hand, a mess of fleshy debris. 'John Grobian and his sons own this road, or so they say. You should find another way if you can.'

'You should have paid the Way Knights' fee,' Goodkin told them.

'We did.' The old man took off his hat respectfully. 'Grobian's sons were making bloody sport of our Way Knights when we escaped! I ain't never seen such cruelty before. By the Goddess, I can still hear their screams in my head!'

'Who's Grobian?' Daimonia asked.

'John Grobian used to be an enforcer in the pay of the prince. Did all kinds of dirty work not appropriate for knights. Enjoyed it too, from what I hear. But there was some kind of violent disagreement and Grobian ended up on the other side of the Accord. Course he still had all the men and weapons he'd been supplied with.'

Daimonia's eyes were on the groaning boy, who met her stare with something like need. She climbed over onto their caravan and stroked his curly hair from his face.

'There's nothing to be done for him now.' The old man sighed.

'Is he your friend?'

'My son.' He smiled weakly. 'He's always been mad about stories of knights and adventure. I tried to get him to read sensible books, but he wouldn't have any of it. Silly boy imagined he wouldn't be a real man if he didn't stand up to those Grobians.'

Daimonia's fingers were warm and red as she drew away from the dying youth. She looked wide-eyed at Goodkin, who stared expressionlessly from his mount.

'You will be avenged, I swear it!' Daimonia squeezed the young man's arm. 'Let's go, Goodkin. Hopefully your brothers-in-arms are still alive. I'm keen to see what happens when these brigands pit their will against yours!'

'No.' Goodkin was unmoved. 'We've travelled far enough tonight. We camp here.'

'What?' Daimonia's brows knotted into a fierce curl. 'Your own comrades are left to the mercy of robbers and you want to sleep?'

'Now, now,' Svek intervened. 'Goodkin's job is to keep us alive. Not to avenge every crime on the journey. Let us take rest with these fellows and we will all be the safer for it.'

'No offense, but we must continue,' the old man told them. 'The company of Way Knights is seen as provocation to Grobian's boys. That much I learnt today and shall never forget.'

'Why is everyone ignoring the truth?' Daimonia looked to each man, her head turning quickly like a bird's. 'What if those knights were being murdered right here in front of us? Would you ignore it then?'

'I'll care when it's happening to me or my family,' Purtur interjected. 'What's the sense in getting killed over other people's disputes?'

'If my mother were here, she would not stand idly by.'

'Come on, girl!' Purtur waved away her assertion. 'Female knights are for parades not wars. And war is what we'll have if we start killing the sons of Grobian.'

Goodkin had already dismounted and was preparing to camp. He cared for his wounded horse, tenderly stroking the beast's head and whispering encouragement. Daimonia marched over and stood in his way, hands on hips, head tilted to the side questioningly.

116

'What does it mean to be a Way Knight?' she challenged, thumping her fist on his armour.

'We persevere.' Goodkin told her. He took off his helmet as if his face would fend her off. 'We persevere or die.'

'I'm going to help those knights.' She began to turn, still meeting the Way Knight's stare. 'I'm going and you'll be forced to help me.'

'No, I won't.' He took a silver piece from his purse and offered it back to the girl. 'Take it and leave if you must.'

Daimonia's hand hovered tentatively over the coin, but she made a fist instead and struck the Way Knight in the mouth.

Goodkin flinched in surprise, wiping his lips with the back of his gauntlet. There was a sliver of blood between his teeth. The encampment fell to silence as everyone looked aghast at the knight and the girl. Hem was shaking and Fletcher led his children hurriedly away from the scene.

Goodkin growled at his attacker. Hurt swam in his eyes but quickly fermented into bitterness. 'I told you. Provoke no enemy.' Angrily he threw the silver denarius into the sky; it lit like a star for a moment and then disappeared into the deep wood.

Daimonia stared at the knight unapologetically, her chest rising with hot breaths.

'Let's everyone calm down,' Hem suggested. But Daimonia had already gone, following the trail of the coin.

The Sons of Grobian

Daimonia had never named the dead watchman's horse. The beast's history was too unknown, its journeys indiscoverable. More than that, she never felt the horse belonged to her, in the way that some horses and their riders seem joined. Not until tonight.

'Chrestos,' she called him, smoothing his mane and the barbarian muscles of his back. 'Chrestos, guide me through the night.'

She didn't need Goodkin or any of them. They were like scripted actors, stuck in their roles, not even aware they were alive. She let them fall away from her mind, like floundering ghosts, as she rode.

The warlike thump of Chrestos' hooves was the pounding of her heart. Storming through the darkness, an exhilarating freedom blew through her soul. Where was she going now? Perhaps she had no destination. She unsheathed the watchman's sword and let it slice through the night. She was Cere-Thalatte, riding into battle, the avenging Goddess despoiling her foes! A terrible laughter filled the night, erupting from some secret place within.

'I am the flaming sword!' she rejoiced. She rode on, smelting her anger into steel, until at last she found her prey.

In a wooded clearing the torso of a dead horse roasted over a greedy fire. The Grobians camped openly around the warming flame; drunk as militants, they snored into their shabby beards. There were almost a dozen men, surrounded by axes, swords and spears. Discarded armour and clothes were strewn about.

Two prisoners were kept here. A blood-drenched Way Knight staggered pitifully around the campsite, as far as his noose would allow. A crude mask of spiked metal was clamped tightly around his head. He roared agonisingly as blood leaked from the device and flowed down his crimson tabard. Desperately, he thrashed and jerked, trying to throw himself into the fire.

Another Way Knight had been stripped and tied to a tree, his skin pouring with sweat. His wavering cries encouraged a young torturer, who worked on the knight's body.

The young Grobian had an inordinately fat head, thick limbs and haphazardly chopped hair. He swaggered, arms held out to exaggerate his biceps, as if the forest were too small for anyone but himself. From the waist down he was naked, his speckled bottom bulging obtrusively.

Crouched in the shadows with her weapons, Daimonia felt terror beat against the armour of her heart. She nurtured the inner fire she had kindled. *Give me one moment of courage*, she prayed. *No, not courage. Give me one moment of truth!*

Nocking an arrow, she followed the movements of the Grobian youth with her bow. His swaying belly made a large, if moving target. She stared at his neck, which was ringed with a bone necklace. A silent kill was needed if she were to rescue the tortured knights and not wake the camp.

She loosed the arrow with a prayer. Already her hands were reaching instinctively for a second.

119

The Grobian turned at that moment and the arrow missed him, sticking the tied Way Knight in the face. The knight screamed hideously and whacked his head against the tree as if to force the shaft from his skull. Blood spurted from the agonising wound as he ground his jaws and contorted his face, his cries terrifying the birds from the trees.

Daimonia's fingers became numb. She dropped the next arrow, gasping with horror as it disappeared into the leaves. She drew another, fighting a sudden dizziness as the young Grobian spun this way and that to determine the arrow's source.

Daimonia drew again and let fly. The arrow landed firmly between the youth's plump buttocks. He leapt into the air with a howl, his hands flapping at his rear as he danced manically.

Awakened and agitated, the other Grobians were rising and unsheathing weapons. Each man's hair was shorn in a berserk style, with faces painted to exaggerate their ferocity.

'Kill them!' the arse-pierced youth was roaring at the forest. He was on all fours now like a pig, his inner thighs wet with blood and excrement. Daimonia shot him again and then again. He lifted his head and squealed as the arrows ruptured his flesh, straining furiously against death.

Nervous laughter tittered from Daimonia's lips. Even as vigilant torches approached, the image of the strained face was fixed in her mind's eye.

She turned and dipped into the undergrowth, prowling forward like a serpent. She had played this game as a child with Niklos, hiding from each other in the woods. Sliding across the mossy ground on her belly, she made herself a slight and silent snake.

'Come out and fight, you arse-baiting cowards!' someone was blustering. The Grobians were readying for a score of foes. Shields were hammered provocatively and curses filled the air.

'Can you run?' Daimonia slid up behind the masked Way Knight, who had slumped to his knees. She reached through the atrocious torture mask to soothe his face. He was a young man, bony and lean, not a slab of gritty rock like Goodkin.

'I beg you,' he groaned through the metal. 'Give me one chance to set loose on these dogs!'

'You can escape,' Daimonia assured him. 'No need to die.' She took the Visoth dagger to his noose and tried to cut. The rope was thick and unyielding and she split her thumb before succeeding.

The Grobians' ire was rising. They howled like war wolves, barking obscenities into the deathly darkness. Their painted faces were grim or else exhibiting extraordinarily violent expressions. Goading attack, they probed the fringes of their camp with axes and swords.

'Quick.' Daimonia beckoned.

Instead the young Way Knight seized Daimonia's sword and charged at the Grobian pack, yelling, 'Revenge!' Hate gave ferocity to his strikes. Men crumpled and screamed, clasping at grievous gashes and mangled limbs.

Daimonia watched the war-madness with lurid excitement, her heart close to bursting. She reached for her bow and tried to shoot the Grobians in the back, but the men had seen her, and as the masked Way Knight succumbed to their swords, they came for her.

The Corpse Returns

As a child Hem had been plagued with nightmares, having been told once too many times that the Burning Man would take him if he didn't behave. In one especially vivid dream Gorach Baoth stood by his bed and gloated, claiming Hem as his own. That same night he had awoken to a far more dismaying scene: his parents rutting greedily in the dark.

In troubled times Hem's mother would soothe his fears with her kisses. She would stroke his face and smile reassuringly. Her smile could dispel the scariest dream or heal a bloody knee. But tonight Hem's mother was all the way back home in Littlecrook and a thing was out to get him. Something made of wrinkled flesh and old lust that wanted to fill Hem's holes; a thing that called itself Svek and pretended to be a man.

During the day, the Svek-thing had been skewing Hem with its stare. Goddess only knew what depravities it was imagining. At least its interest had drifted away from the Fletcher children, although some cowardly part of Hem wished it was them instead of him.

Tonight Hem needed to stay close to the others, no matter how badly his bowels rumbled. He needed to be near the Way Knight, where he might be safe. The thing called Svek had wandered off with a wink and a chuckle, and Hem was convinced it would return to take him.

122

Hem made a bed close to his father, who met the boy's needy look with a withering stare and rolled over. He lay on his back, watching the sinister stars; from the vantage of space they presided over all mysteries and secrets. The stars alone knew the truth.

Within too short a time everyone was asleep, deep in comforting dreams, while Hem remained awake to every sound of the forest. They had left Hem alone to survive the night.

Something began to crawl from the woods. Hem began blubbering in distress. His eyes filled with tears as, lying petrified, he waited for Svek to come twisting and shuddering into view. Instead he saw Pickle grabbing fistfuls of flowers and pulling them up from the grass.

'What are you doing?' Hem hissed at the child.

'Daisies,' she said, showing the little collection in her palm.

'Go back to your mother,' Hem demanded. The Fletchers were camped together in the next clearing. 'You must go back to sleep!'

'Don't want to,' Pickle protested. She pulled an obstinate expression, her lips pouting sulkily.

'You must,' Hem insisted. He slapped her hand to emphasise the point but immediately felt regret. Pickle's eyes welled with tears, but much to Hem's relief, she ran back to her family.

Looking around the camp, another fear made Hem's stomach roll and rumble. Where was Daimonia? Purtur had predicted she would slink back apologetically during the night, and no one but Hem had seemed the least bit concerned by her outburst. They had laughed it off as girlish petulance.

But Hem saw something different in Daimonia. She was a sword waiting to be drawn, a spirit unconstrained by the conventions binding the others. She had hit Goodkin in the face and challenged the Seidhr! She was not going to live very long.

Where was she going? Surely she didn't intend to confront the Grobians, about whom she had made so much fuss. What if she ran into the Svek-thing?

Fanciful scenarios played out in Hem's imagination. Daimonia would be confronted by Svek and Hem would save her. Grateful, she would hold him in her slender arms and lay her face against his chest. Becoming aware of his manhood, she would slip from her dress and they would couple secretly in the dark. *I love you*, she would whisper as he emptied inside her.

Instead of that adventure, Hem remained where he lay, unable to move. His limbs were heavy as stone and his breath had become wheezing. He turned his head to squint at the sleeping Way Knight. It seemed unsafe to stare at Goodkin when the knight was awake, but Hem was continually drawn to the thickly scarred face. A nauseating feeling filled his gut, but it was not disgust at Goodkin's disfigurements. Instead Hem felt disgusted with himself; he was soft, fat and scared. He could never be a man like Goodkin, a man who was probably tough from birth. He would never be the kind of man who could help Daimonia.

Then he heard it, the awful laugh.

The Svek-thing was by the horses, its saggy face gleeful as it played with them. Hem vomited up the last of his courage and felt his heart freeze as the thing turned its gaze right at him. It licked its fingers before

124

picking its way among the sleepers in exaggerated grotesque steps. Completely naked, it had discarded its deceptive wig and respectable clothes. Flesh dangled and swung, its excitement rising visibly as it smelled the boy's fear and crouched over him.

Around Hem, the others slept as soundly as children. Why could no one see what was happening to him? There was a predator in their midst, who may as well have been invisible. Hem tried to roar, to wake the very stars, but all that came out was a pitiful bleat.

The Svek-thing smiled, wrinkles slithering around its face. It stroked Hem's lips, taking time to be gentle as its slick wet fingers probed affectionately. Together they seemed to slip into a secret place unknown to the others, a place where Hem would no longer be Hem but the object of the thing's desires.

'Please,' Hem gasped weakly. If only there were a way he could show the thing who he truly was, all his loves and cares, all his memories, it would surely leave him alone. 'Please, you don't know me.'

It slipped its tongue between Hem's teeth and explored his mouth greedily, the indulgent and invasive act imposing the Svek-thing's vision of Hem over the real one.

Hem remembered his warm home and the smell of the flowers in the garden. He recalled the sight of his mother waving them away on their journey as the dog chased them down the path. His mother had worn her brightest smile, lighting up his world, but Hem knew she would be lonely until they returned. Hem and his mother often knew each other's thoughts, could laugh together like no one else could imagine, until Hem would lay on the floor exhausted and the dog would run up and lick his face. Lying alone in her bed, would Hem's mother know he was in trouble now?

The thing was writhing frantically, its jaws wide with panic. Behind it stood the Way Knight with his powerful fingers pressed against the creature's eyes. The Svek-thing shook and tried to claw itself loose, but Goodkin slowly increased the pressure until his fingertips were deep in Svek's eye sockets. Mucous drizzled down its blinded face.

'Move,' Goodkin told Hem.

Hem rolled away as Goodkin knelt on the writhing, shrieking thing's back and forced it against the bedroll. He pulled a weighty mace from his belt and, with slow deliberation, broke apart the Svek-thing's skull like he was carefully cracking some rocks.

Purtur, finally awake, began retching at the sight and stumbled away to the trees.

Hem examined himself; he was alive! He had messed himself but was able to breathe again. In just a few weeks he would be back in his mother's arms. His heart soared at the thought as enormous relief washed over him. He promised he would be more appreciative of her this time, no more reluctance to help with the chores or to take the dog out.

He went to offer thanks to Goodkin, but the knight was looking around the camp with urgent turns of his ugly head.

'Where's the girl?' the knight growled.

Hem felt ashamed and confused. 'She's gone. You saw her go! We all did!'

'I thought that–' Goodkin looked about ready to bite his own face

126

off. He grabbed his shield and swung onto his horse, riding off with as much thunder as a cavalry charge.

Hem looked at the Svek-thing's corpse and a sudden courage lifted him. He pulled the bloody mace from the debris and hefted its weight in his hands.

'What you going to do with that?' Purtur snapped. He was wiping his face clean with his tunic sleeve.

'I'm going to help Daimonia,' Hem asserted.

'If that girl has run off, then let her die. I don't like her anyway and it ain't our concern. And what are you going to do anyway, you useless fat idiot?'

'I'm not useless!' Hem rose out of his slouch, rising to his full height above his father. Then he was off, jogging down the road, through the uncertain shadows. Within an incredibly short time he was out of breath, struggling to do more than fall from one foot to the next.

He walked back exhaustedly to the sound of his father's derisive snorts.

'You're no Way Knight,' Purtur mocked.

'I am today,' Hem replied. He untethered his faithful cart-horse and wrenched himself onto her back. 'Come on, Gertsie,' he coaxed. 'Let's find Daimonia.' The horse was uninterested in moving, struggling to adjust to Hem's weight on her back. Then, finding it preferable to the cart, Gertsie rushed ahead into the wood.

Allowed to run at speed, Gertsie eagerly made ground on the Way Knight's horse until they were riding neck and neck. Goodkin's expression turned from consternation to bewilderment as Hem pulled ahead and overtook him.

'Idiot!' Goodkin's croaky voice chased them. 'Bloody stupid idiot!'

Hem allowed a wild grin to take over his face. This was his night now. 'Faster, Gertsie,' he encouraged, half-daft with exhilaration. Even in the rushing wind he could clearly hear shouts and clashes in the air. He made for them determinedly as Gertsie bore him along.

'Daimonia!' he called out. His voice lacked power and he tried again. 'DAIMONIA!' He put all of his wind into it.

And then Daimonia was there, breaking out from the trees and running towards him. Hem could see the fear in her large eyes as she sprinted desperately. This was it, he told himself, riding keenly to the rescue. *This is my moment.* A second later all courage shrivelled as a gang of warpainted maniacs leapt from the forest, spitting murderous curses as they pursued the girl.

Hem wrestled with the impulse to retreat and hurry all the way back home to Littlecrook. Despite his best intentions, he began pulling back on the reins in panic.

Daimonia fell, her hair whipping out as she stumbled and struck the ground, scraping her palms and knees. The men laughed, the fastest throwing himself atop the girl with all his muscled weight. They wrestled in the dirt as the outlaws gathered about with jeers and protruding tongues.

Behind them strode a colossus of a man, a puffed-out warrior whose outstretched gait exaggerated his size even further. The warrior was beardless but wore his hair in thick black braids. Over his shoulder he carried a monstrous hammer, while his other hand scooped around his crotch in a vulgar gesture of virility.

'Best let John 'ave her first,' one of the others warned as the giant pushed in amongst them.

Goodkin's horse broke into the crowd in a fit of hooves and metal. The bone-crunching impact sent bodies sprawling in all directions. A chaotic barrage of slashing, stabbing attacks rained down as the Grobians fell over each other to get clear.

Hem found himself riding forward; it was happening without conscious choice, but he was moving towards the savage fight, rushing into the fray. He saw Daimonia burst from the earth, stabbing her attacker around the throat and face with ferocious hatred.

Big John Grobian was the first to recover from the collision. He swung his weighty hammer at Goodkin, shattering his shield and dismounting the Way Knight in a shower of splintered wood.

Hem rode straight for the huge man and walloped him in the head with the mace. The man's nose seemed to disappear, as if his face had been turned inside out. Hem shook his fist in triumph.

'Boy, look out!' Daimonia shouted.

John Grobian retaliated, his mallet finding Hem's skull with the sound of metal on meat. The world went black then thick red as the sky changed places with the earth. As Hem looked up at the hammer-wielding giant, a strange thought crossed his mind. Did Daimonia even know his name? He was about to die for her and she had called him *boy*.

But then it didn't matter because there was his mother. There was that smile, the one that told Hem everything was perfect.

Scars upon Scars

'Sometimes you will need to kill,' Jhonan had once told Daimonia. It had been a sharp winter morning when the whole of Jaromir was blighted by a drift of snow. From the vantage of the old watchtower they had observed the villagers trying to get about, little shapes struggling through the sun-glazed white.

'I don't want to be a knight,' Daimonia had told him, hugging herself against the cold. 'I don't want to fight, I want to learn. I want to understand everything.'

'Violence will choose you,' Jhonan warned. 'Whether you seek it or not.'

'If ever it does, I will run straight to you.' She smiled, drinking up her grandfather's ardent protectiveness. Falling snowflakes nestled in her ebony hair, making a pale crown before melting.

Jhonan allowed his eyes to soften without smiling. He tried to stroke the girl's shoulder, but he was awkward, unnatural with affection. 'I won't be here forever.' He leaned close, the drink on his breath poisoning the air. 'And what of your own children and grandchildren? Who will keep them from harm?'

'I'll never be a mother, nor a wife!' Daimonia's mischievous smile gave her face warmth. 'No man could bear all my questions!'

'Imagine you had your own girl,' Jhonan persisted. 'A child you loved more than all else. A little Daimonia with big curious eyes and a frown.' He cradled an imaginary infant. 'What would you do if she were threatened? What if someone did violence against her? How would you answer your enemies?'

Daimonia felt a flare of emotion searing away the cold. Although she knew Jhonan was baiting her, her heart still felt like a hot coal. Her answer was thoughtful but emphatic. 'There is nothing that could be done to me or mine that I wouldn't repay worse in return.'

Jhonan's face hardened. If he felt discomfort, it quickly became resolution. 'Then learn,' he told her, drawing the knife from his belt. 'Learn and be ready.'

Tonight the forest was the stage of terrible cruelty. Hem's corpse lay sprawled upon the earth, surrounded by wet mess. Men crawled amid their own guts, hacking up the last breaths of life.

Daimonia was drenched in sweat and blood, her dress stuck to her body. A supernatural anger roared through her brain. She was possessed, a weapon of chaos, unable to think but only to act. Her Visoth dagger was rose red as she wrenched it from the neck of her attacker. She took her blade to other men as they tried to rise, using her weight to puncture leather and flesh.

Goodkin climbed to his feet shakily, his shield in bits around him. He gripped his sword in both hands as John Grobian charged. The great hammer swung from sky to earth, fetching a clod of mud into the air as Goodkin leapt aside. The Way Knight drove his blade to the giant's neck, but the attack was broken by an intercepting kick. The massive foot propelled Goodkin backwards and the hammer swung again, glancing Goodkin's helm with a resounding clang.

Another Grobian fighter seized the moment to chop at Goodkin with his war axe. His reckless attacks were as audacious as his warpaint, which depicted the cock of Chrestos on his chest. The lunatic howled as his axe clashed against the knight's mail. Goodkin leapt into a powerful headbutt, breaking the Grobian's skull with his helm.

John Grobian barked out a series of rutting noises as he hefted his hammer in a great arc, forcing the Way Knight to retreat. Goodkin threw his sword at Grobian, pursuing it with a charge. The giant dropped his weapon and both men met in a wrestler's grip. Their faces contorted as they strained to gain advantage, eyes bulging and teeth grinding. Their hands clenched around each other's veined and reddening throats.

John Grobian's strength prevailed. His powerful arms swelled as he forced Goodkin down to his crotch with a gloating cluck. Daimonia ran to Goodkin's aid, but the giant swatted her away, splitting her lips like crushed fruit.

As Grobian watched the girl fall, Goodkin drew back his arm and stove his gauntleted fist into the big man's testicles. Grobian crumpled, hacking snot and blood down his face.

Goodkin pulled off his helm and fought for breath, sweat streaming down the tracks of his scars. He took up the discarded war axe and with a roar brought it down on John Grobian's neck. The head rolled to land upright on the ground, staring at Daimonia.

'We did it,' Daimonia gasped.

'Did what?' Goodkin growled. 'Got Hem's brains smashed in? Look at him! This is your doing!'

Daimonia's lips trembled. The spirit of war was fading and all there was to see were dead men and a foolish boy's unrecognisable head.

'Curse you, Daimonia,' Goodkin spat. 'I should never have allowed a Vornir in my company. All Vornirs are animals and, from what I hear, traitors!'

Daimonia ran at him with the dagger. She lunged for the terrible face as Goodkin raised his forearm to block the strike. The Way Knight had underestimated her skill and the dagger scratched across his face, opening an earlier scar.

Daimonia cried out, as if it were she who bore the wound. Goodkin seized her wrist and pulled her sweaty body against his, bringing the blade to the girl's throat.

'I told you not to leave me.' His eyes watered. 'I told you not to provoke enemies!'

'I'm not your property.' She twisted and pulled away.

'We had a contract.'

'I'll go the rest of the way alone.'

'No. Here's what you'll do. You'll help me take Hem back to Purtur. You'll look after his body until we can find an adjurator. And you'll do nothing, nor say a single word until we reach Khorgov and go our separate ways.'

Their enemies were left to the crows, a grievous insult among the Dallish. No one had the inclination to see they received the final rites. The Svek-thing was thrown into a ditch where even the Goddess might not find it.

A day later Hem and the two young Way Knights were burned on the hill above Chalkwater. Smoke bellowed into the immense ocean of sky above, where a tumult of thunder answered the departing spirits. The rustle of flames offered a peculiar calm.

Purtur was on his knees, drawn up into himself. Around him the Fletcher family gathered supportively, the children's energy temporarily subdued by the alluring pillars of fire. They would travel no further with Goodkin's company.

The Way Knight stood beside them, his helm removed respectfully and his head lowered in respect. It was clear he counted it a personal shame to lose a life on the journey. He had ensured his dead comrades were burned in their Way Knight tabards, saving one of their shields to replace his own.

Daimonia felt bruised and unwanted. Tenderness had replaced the furnace in her heart, and she was weak again, limp and cold. The ritual droned on, but she did not listen to the babbling words of the adjurator. The real prayer was around her in smoke, storm and sky.

Wanderers on the Vale

A slender virgin walked through the twilight as eager shadows stroked her body. She carried a flaming sword before her, gripping its handle firmly with both hands. Her arms were painted black and stained with trickles of candle wax; her hair was extraordinarily long and topped with a wooden crown. The ever-burning weapon illuminated her rapturous expression and the intense fervour of her eyes. She wandered continually onward as if in a dream.

The virgin was followed by a long train of Thalattist monks trudging dutifully through the vale, one hundred devotees following the winding river. Each wore a modest habit tied with a woollen belt and had long hair, uncut since initiation. They carried ceremonial weapons: a bow, dagger or sword as required by the Goddess of War. As the holy warriors journeyed, they repeated the sacred chant of their order:

Thalatte, Thalatte, bellum dea Thalatte

Nox Thalatte

Bellum dea Thalatte

The Geld Knight Conrad Ernst observed the monks with a kind of admiration. Like him they felt an affinity with the divine. Like him they knew they were special, set apart from the rest of the world. In another life Conrad might have joined them, given himself wholeheartedly to their zealous cult. Like the monks, Conrad understood what it was to need an all-consuming purpose.

Conrad's men were less appreciative. The Geld enforcers laughed at the religious fanatics, but this was to be expected. Such men could not look beyond their basest desires; a connection with the sublime was incomprehensible to them. The oafish Cain went as far as pissing right in the virgin's path. A puddle formed and the Thalattists splashed their bare feet right through it. Conrad predicted the monks would not react to this provocation. Their faith did not permit them to fight until the end times.

The Geld Knight's mouth twisted into an expression of disgust. Not for the first time, Conrad was repulsed by the barbarity of the men he needed to employ. He longed for one more day with his master Pavel and the aesthetes of Kraljevic.

'Cheer up, sir. It's not the end of the world!' Fotter jested.

Conrad resisted the urge to bludgeon Fotter to death. The revolting trapper had become increasingly bold in assuming familiarity with the Geld Knight. Whatever feelings of camaraderie the animal-molester was experiencing were entirely unreciprocated by Sir Conrad. Perhaps the men needed reminding that he was their master.

'Cain.'

'Yes, sir.'

'Come with me.'

Conrad rode out in front of the monks until his horse blocked the path of the sword-wielding virgin. She stared up at him with skull-black eyes and looked ready to strike him from his mount. Behind her the holy warriors lined up, some wearing their anxiety and hatred more obviously than others.

Lumbering up beside the Geld Knight, Cain let out a mischievous cackle.

'Please excuse me,' Conrad told the girl. 'Cain, you seem to have urinated on the holy virgin's feet.'

Cain was almost doubled over with laughter now, holding his stomach as he guffawed.

'Lick them clean,' Conrad commanded.

'But, sir—'

'Do it!' Conrad wore the look of a man barely able to restrain his own fury. He did not have to ask again.

Cain fell to his knees, gagging as he licked the girl's wet toes.

Watching the Thalattists, a kind of revelation descended upon Sir Conrad. What a potent thing religion was for bridling the will of man. These devotees would do anything for their Goddess. They had consecrated their entire lives to mastering her sacred war arts and would voluntarily lay down their lives in her name. Perhaps the Thalattists were an exceptional example, but every peasant from here to Archonia acknowledged some aspect of the Goddess and allowed themselves to be guided by the adjurators.

The merest seed of an idea began to incubate in the Geld Knight's mind. Looking down the long row of monks, Conrad observed their expressions, from the most placid to those whose hatred for the Geld was thinly concealed. His eyes were drawn to a broad pair of shoulders heaving with unbridled emotion.

It occurred to Conrad to try an experiment. He rode over to confront the passionate monk. The young man was firm with years of conditioning in the Thalattist temple; his hair was gathered in an untidy knot and his face was long and resolute like an indignant horse.

'What's your name, boy?' Conrad demanded. Conrad knew these Thalattists did not recognise the authority of the Accord and to compensate he tried to muster his most authoritative voice. Instead he noticed again the nasal quality of his own enunciation, diminishing the command he ought to have.

'Blackthorn,' the strapping warrior told him anyway.

'Well, *Blackthorn.*' Conrad exaggerated the unlikeliness of the name. 'You realise that this little procession is a direct affront to the prince and may be perceived as treason by the courts of Kraljevic?' Conrad leaned back on his horse, allowing a tingle of pleasure to stir his crotch. He was confronting a small army held in check by their convictions. 'Cere-Thalatte is chaos; she is death. Is that what you wish for, boy?'

'With all my heart,' Blackthorn replied insolently. His voice was steady, but his stormy glare and heavy breaths revealed the slayer within.

Conrad lashed out with his horse whip. A crimson gash blemished the youth's handsome face.

An immediate ripple of discontent spread through the line of Thalattists. It was like sticking a pin in a caterpillar. They spat and scowled, some holding back the others, but none lifted a hand against Sir Conrad. The Geld Knight allowed a smug grin to erupt as the young monk was forced to subdue the rage within.

'There is no Goddess,' Conrad informed them. 'There is no Chrestos. There is just us.' Satisfied with their silence, the Geld Knight turned his

138

horse away, but there was a shimmer of movement behind him.

Blackthorn leaped into the air and buried a kick into Conrad's gut. Pain exploded in the Geld Knight's torso and he toppled from his horse with a great expulsion of phlegm. The marsh rushed up to greet his surprised face.

The Geld Knight lay still, his ringed fingers sucked into the muck. It occurred to Conrad that, despite all appearances, this was a kind of victory. He had proved that beneath the pious façade, the religious were just as petty and vindictive as anyone else.

Conrad rose up, his armour again clotted with muck that would require hours of cleaning. His golden hair was in disarray. Nevertheless he wore a look of triumph on his face. Half-smiling, palms open, he gestured in a way that seemed to say *See, I told you so*.

Every Thalattist monk assumed a fighting pose with bow, dagger or sword. Along the vale one hundred warriors stood ready to defend each other.

Conrad laughed. In any ideology there were always clauses and loopholes as to why it was permissible to aggress against enemies. Conrad knew this better than anyone.

The Geld Knight looked to his enforcers. Only the Afreyan had unsheathed his blades, the others preferring to hold themselves or wave their hands in the air as if to ward death away.

'Kill them,' Fotter encouraged the enforcers weakly, although he himself had not drawn a weapon.

Conrad adjusted himself and regained his composure. Once again he had lost face with his uncomprehending men. 'Leave them,' he commanded as if he were sparing the monks' lives. 'This treason will not go unpunished.'

'They will rue the day,' Fotter felt the need to add.

The Geld circuit had led them on a convoluted route, winding from Jaromir to Sophir and then through an even poorer shithole called Muddy Bottom. From there they had crossed the vale heading towards Chalkwater, aiming to arrive in Knave in a few days. The meandering monotony of the journey tried Conrad's patience sorely. How much longer must he endure these mundane duties and humiliations before the Secret God reached out to him?

Along the Chalkwater trail, the distinct smell of death teased Conrad's senses. He was familiar enough with the stink. He had known it all his life from his mother's brutalised corpse to the rotten game they called food in the shires.

'Either something's died around here, or Cain has farted!' Fotter cackled.

Conrad waited while his men examined the scene ahead, no doubt they were helping themselves to any coin or valuables as well.

'All clear, sir,' Scorcher announced. The lad was standing to attention like a dull-witted militant.

Conrad rode ahead lazily to inspect the corpse-streaked trail. A lively battle had been fought here, and since then the animals had enjoyed a charnel feast.

'John Grobian.' Fotter lifted the giant's half-eaten head. 'Had a few drinks with this maniac once. Before he became an enemy of the prince, of course.'

'Maybe he ran into some Way Knights?' Cain suggested, scratching his arse.

'Don't make me laugh!' The Afreyan swordsman strode around the bodies, his eyes darting guardedly into the woods. His tattooed hands clenched the handles of his paired scimitars. 'John Grobian never be falling to some pitiful Way Knights! Must've been something far worser than that!'

Conrad tapped his codpiece, ignoring all the mundane speculation. His mind was oozing possibilities and patterns. An opportunity had fallen into his lap. The clouds drifted and a spear of indescribably brilliant light illuminated the Geld Knight's face. Was the Secret God reaching out to him?

'I want a courier sent to Kraljevic immediately,' Conrad insisted. 'To carry the following message: Geld Knight Conrad Ernst has defeated John Grobian in the prince's name. Put that part about the prince first.'

The scir of Chalkwater flinched at the command. 'Sorry, Sir Conrad, buh-buh-but we have nuh-no courier.' This stuttering refusal was delivered amid a great deal of fidgeting and sweat.

'Then send one of your sons!' Conrad found it was often necessary to state the very obvious to these serfs.

'Buh-but, Sir Conrad,' the scir protested. 'They would nuh-never make the journey alive!'

Conrad shook a goblet of wine in the Chalkwater scir's surprised face. With complete detachment he watched the man's blinking confusion. 'No, I should go personally,' the Geld Knight decided. He would stand before Prince Moranion and present Grobian's head as a trophy.

'Begging your pardon,' the scir's unfortunate-looking daughter interrupted. 'But a terrifying Way Knight passed through here recently.'

'Terrifying?' Conrad raised an eyebrow, half wondering why the slovenly girl was addressing him personally.

'She means Sir Goodkin,' the scir explained. 'A reliable Way Knight buh-but a bit rough on the eye.'

'He must be rough indeed,' Conrad mused, staring at the odd-looking father and daughter.

'I heard it from the adjurators,' the girl continued. 'It was Sir Goodkin killed those Grobians and he left them out there to rot.'

Conrad blinked a few times. He even felt a little tear encroach upon one eye. The implication was clear and all that he had to gain or lose teetered on a single Way Knight and some loose-lipped idiots from Chalkwater.

'What are you doing, my lord!' the scir was shouting.

Conrad's hands had closed around the girl's throat and he was watching her bloated, bewildered face as he squeezed and squeezed the life out of her. The scir was trying to pry them apart and even Fotter had rushed in, trying to extricate Conrad from his madness.

He released the girl and she fell to the floor, gasping desperately. The impressions of the knight's fingers were still hot on her neck.

'I slew John Grobian,' Conrad told the horrified scir. 'Spread the word.'

142

The Silence

Summer winds drifted with the travellers, chasing them through woods and hills, through fords and fertile pastures. From a gusty peak they witnessed lawless horses storming through the uncharted plains. They crunched juicy mouthfuls of apple on a flinty bridge, watching fishes glide through their reflections. Beyond the veil of a waterfall an immense stone brooded like a giant's discarded head.

They passed strange wanderers, considered wise for their homes were the boundless land itself and they paid no taxes. They met outlaws ganged together in crude families, parading beards and weapons like a priesthood of thieves. The Way Knight was the shield against which these strangers would not test their courage.

Goodkin knew the territory like an old enemy to be sought out and reconquered. He never lost his way nor flinched through storm or flood. His scars were the only map he referred to, sometimes probing the valleys of his flesh with gauntleted fingers.

Despite the wild beauty, Daimonia followed as if through a mausoleum. Ghosts accumulated in the crypt of her imagination, spectral accusers following her progress. Her beloved Niklos was now joined by the knights she had failed to rescue and the foolish son of Purtur. Their funeral had submerged her vindictive passions and birthed

143

confusion and regret. Who was she to challenge and defy? She was not Cere-Thalatte or even Captain Catherine.

Daimonia drove the second cart, avoiding Purtur as best she could, though their party had shrunk to three. Bereaved beyond words, the merchant had become a thing Daimonia feared to see. His face seemed to cave beneath his brows, morose like failing clay.

Beyond her frailty of heart, Daimonia was also less practically prepared for the travails of the journey than she had imagined. Her frayed and blood-blotched dress offered faint protection during the shivery nights. At times she even wished the Way Knight would hold her in the dark. Instead he remained distant and cold, hiding behind his wound-masked face.

'My grandfather bears a scar from the side of his mouth to the hollow of his ear,' Daimonia told Goodkin one night when Purtur was asleep. The Way Knight had allowed a campfire and the warm radius of light made a discreet chamber in the woods. 'Many of grandfather's fingers look like little nailless toes,' she continued when the Way Knight made no acknowledgement. 'He has many war wounds.'

Goodkin did not respond to these enticements to speak, except to fix the girl with a deathly stare. He lay against a towering ash, his fists clenched like a child refusing to part with a toy.

'I imagine you must have some stories to tell,' Daimonia tried again. She gestured to her own relatively unblemished face. A scar had formed across her lips, but her bruises were now mild discolourations.

'We're not friends,' he told her abruptly. 'Neither am I some curiosity for you to enjoy.'

Daimonia hid her embarrassment behind her tattered sleeve. The Way Knight had caught her presumption, exposing her implacable curiosity, which had already been the source of so much sorrow. Nevertheless she felt herself moved to anger. Who was this man to presume his suffering was so much greater than hers? What of all she had lost? Might yet lose?

'You're not the only one in pain!' She returned his harsh stare. 'My brother was murdered and my love for him was beyond the horizons of all the roads you've ever travelled!'

'Do not,' the Way Knight told her, raising his palm like a shield.

'Do not what?'

'Do not try to draw me into your story,' he growled. 'Do not try to know mine. We have an agreement, a simple contract; that and nothing more.'

Daimonia bit at her lip and dug her nails into her skin as her heart broke away from her. 'You must have loved once,' she managed to reply, a little weepily.

Goodkin's expression transformed from stone to astonishment. His scars created unfamiliar patterns around his eyes and mouth. It seemed the exchange was completely off the path.

For the longest time only the fire had voice, consuming the weathered wood with a fervent crackle.

'Passengers.' Goodkin broke the silence. 'That's what we call you. Those who pay the Way Knight's fee in return for our protection.'

Daimonia said nothing in case she might spoil Goodkin's willingness to speak. Instead she sat attentively, wrapping her cloak about her.

'I've had passengers die before,' he told her flatly. 'Sometimes all of them. Whole families falling prey to raiders or harsh conditions. I've had passengers steal from me, try to deceive me, even try to kill me. There is pain at the beginning, but you learn. You learn to feel nothing.'

'I think you're wrong,' Daimonia challenged.

Goodkin looked incredulous. 'What?'

'I think it is you who are the passenger. I have purpose, a cause, and you exist only to accompany me on it. I am alive with hopes and vulnerabilities and, yes, with pain. But you who feel nothing' – she raised a trembling hand to point at the knight – 'you are dead!'

The Slaughter Gardens

'This world is a story and our lives nothing more than the musings of a playwright.' The white-haired speaker was perched upon a broad tree stump, his hands working as if fashioning an invisible pot. 'It feels like we have free choice, but most of us cannot divert our own stories once the initial stage is set.' A crowd clustered around the speaker, some making the sign of agreement while others booed and laughed.

Across from the old man a glaring woman tried to sway the crowd to her own tree stump. 'Each of us is the captain of our own ship,' she argued. 'We decide the destination and choose the course.' A good many listeners agreed with her while others floated between the two stumps. 'We have both choice and accountability,' the woman concluded. 'No good blaming our problems on anyone else.'

Daimonia followed Goodkin and Purtur through the busy garden. She wondered at the fervent disagreement, noting that each competing voice seemed compelling and sincere.

'I was a drunkard, a whoremonger and a thief,' a new speaker admitted, taking his place on a stump. 'My wife had left me and my children would not speak to me. I became a spice addict, living on the streets and hurting people just to get a few denarii. I frightened little children, stole from temples and was generally the most unlovable shit imaginable. But then Chrestos gave me rest in his shadow. He chose me to shout his holy words at you.'

A derisive laugh cut the air. 'The gods are nothing more than images of parental authority,' a man replied. 'Symbols designed to keep us obedient and to stop us thinking!'

'Who are all these people?' Daimonia asked.

'Idiots!' Purtur sneered. Arriving at the thriving town of Knave had reawakened him. 'The Slaughter Gardens used to be a place for the condemned to make a last speech before execution. Now the whole place is overrun with pointless arguments and debates!'

'How can I make sense of all these ideas?' Daimonia wondered. 'By what means should I accept or reject the arguments?'

'Eh? What?' Purtur scratched his head.

'Some know in their hearts what is true,' said Daimonia. 'While others say that ideas must be tested.'

'I just use my own common sense.' Purtur yawned. 'As long as you have food in your belly, there ain't any need to wrestle with all these philosophies.'

Daimonia frowned. 'A good question is better than a poor answer.' She turned to the Way Knight. 'What do you believe?'

Goodkin looked away, searching the crowd for dangers.

'The Accord is a lie!' someone was yelling.

'Hah!' Purtur snorted. 'Sounds like someone has just made their last speech!'

The speaker was a young man whose pronounced brow and protruding lower lip gave him a look of determined defiance. 'The

Accord is a lie!' he insisted. 'We've warred with the other princedoms so that the Guldslags can grow rich, selling swords and spears to both sides! We've provoked the Baoth, raiding their islands for resources, and when they retaliate, we call *them* barbarians! We live in a time when the Duke of Khorgov paid a thousand denarii for a single hat while others can't even afford to eat! Why is this allowed to happen?' Words poured hurriedly from the youth's mouth as if they might be stopped at any moment. 'The so-called nobles want us to blame petty criminals, the poor and Visoth migrants for all the problems they themselves have caused. The prince wants us to hate each other while he drinks the sweat of our labour and the blood of our sons!'

Some were ignited by the young man's speech, while others booed and made the sign of the crucified traitor with their fingers.

'No one is disputing the prince's lack of virtue,' a bushy-browed elder responded. 'A virtuous prince would be weak. He would be crushed by his enemies. A prince must be ruthless and strong; he must demonstrate his superiority to other men.'

'You freely admit the prince lacks virtue,' the young man replied. 'Why then do you consider it right and proper to obey him and abide by the Accord?'

A squad of militants shoved through the crowd, advancing on the youth from each direction. Upon seeing them, he laughed and threw his arms around the first to reach him, shouting, 'Hug a militant!' They dragged him off and beat him with their clubs until his face swelled and his hands dangled loosely from his wrists.

'Stop them!' Daimonia shouted, already fighting her way towards the men.

'No!' Purtur tried to grab her sleeve, but she was already gone, leaving him holding a fragment of lace. 'Stupid girl!' the merchant called despairingly after her. 'Come back, you bloody idiot!'

The militants began to heft the youth into a carriage cage whilst he writhed against their efforts. Daimonia threw herself into the scene. Trying to protect the young man with her own body, she seized him in a tight hug. 'I won't let them take you, brother!' she said.

The boy was not her brother, but he held her just as tightly for a warm moment. Daimonia's thoughts lingered on a heartbreaking memory: she and Niklos cuddling by the fireplace at Vornir Manor. She clung to the boy, as if to the past, until the militants wrenched them abruptly apart.

'Get off!' Daimonia protested, trying to pull free. She recoiled at the hardness of the men's expressions; their faces seemed devoid of life, like flesh decorating bone.

One militant put a hand under Daimonia's chin and the other on the back of her head. He twisted her neck, forcing the girl to the ground, where the other men began to bend her legs and arms.

'I'll kill you!' she screamed as they incapacitated her. A boot pressed down on the back of her head, making her swallow the earth. She tried to draw a breath but could not force her face back. 'Help!' she blubbered into the mud.

She burst free to see Goodkin in the midst of the men, battering them with his shield. A guttural roar erupted from the Way

Knight's throat as he beat them back energetically. Each savage strike led to another from shield, elbow and fist. He was a beast within armour, striking wildly with no thought of defence.

The militants wailed and tumbled like chastised children. Surrounding debates ceased as the whole crowd became entirely focused on the brawl. The spectators' faces raged as if they themselves struggled in the fight.

The militants were caught off guard, one man freezing even before Goodkin smashed a gauntlet into his stupefied face. Another was crouched low, protecting his head with his arms and trying to scurry away. Goodkin drove his armoured boot right into the coward's backside.

More militants were ploughing through the crowd, clustered together like a many-headed beast. Their white-haired leader shoved gawking peasants out of his way and strode up to confront Goodkin. The man's rank was apparent from the hefty pauldrons that exaggerated his shoulders. He was a sergeant, a veteran with a knowing, canny look.

'Right then, you dirty chitter.' The sergeant's voice had the low authority of a common street thug. 'Get your foot out of Vlad's arse before I hack it off and shove it down your neck.'

Goodkin took a single step forwards. He pulled off his helm and spat blood from his mouth. The crowd did not react as badly to his ruined face as they might have done. Many were encouraging him to further violence, daring him to piss or shit on the defeated men.

Daimonia found herself holding to Goodkin's arm; she was trembling and fixed herself to the steadfastness of her armoured protector. Metal and muscle felt firm beneath her fingers. However, the boy she had tried to save had gone, scarpered away in the melee. Once again the consequences of her intervention were rolling out of control.

'I apologise,' Goodkin stated thickly.

The sergeant looked confused and suspicious. 'You what?'

'I did my duty.' He nodded to Daimonia. 'To protect my passenger, the girl.'

The crowd were unhappy with this exchange, their blood roused to see more violence. Some shouted, 'Coward!' Others called, 'Fight! Fight! Fight!'

'I'll pay the fine.' Goodkin threw a pouch of coin to the sergeant. He parted with the money as if it was a small matter, but his unblinking stare warned against any further incitement.

The sergeant grabbed the pouch and squeezed it in his palm. 'Coin'll soothe some wounds,' he said. 'But it won't pay for your crime. For violence against the Duke's militants you face either thirty days or thirty lashes.'

'Lashes,' Goodkin decided.

'Better you choose the days.' The sergeant offered a rueful smile. 'Men fail under the lash. They cry and soil themselves. They die.'

'And what of these men?' Daimonia pointed to the injured militants, who were rising from the mud, checking their teeth and bruises. 'What penalty does the Accord prescribe for their violence?'

'They were doing their duty.' The sergeant looked affronted. 'And now I'll perform mine. But if you want to make a speech about it, you've come to the right place.' The sergeant looked to the dispersing crowd. People were already hurrying off to secure a good view for the lashing.

The militants grabbed Goodkin's shield and stripped him of weapons. They pulled off his gauntlets and fastened his wrists so tightly that his hands looked ripe to burst.

Goodkin turned to Daimonia. 'Stay with Purtur. I'll find you.'

Daimonia had only the vaguest sense of what the lashes would involve, but she understood that Goodkin was to be brutalised for her sake. No reason or argument would circumvent these men, their law and the violence at their disposal. She shook with anger and futility, wishing she had the power to assert her own justice.

'Stupid girl!' Purtur's face was sour. 'I'd have left you in the dirt!' He bravely wedged himself between the militants to offer Goodkin a swig of ale. 'Perhaps our ugly Way Knight has soft feelings for the pretty girl?'

'I feel nothing,' Goodkin replied bitterly. 'I am dead.'

The Hurting Post

'What's wrong with you?' Purtur was shaking like a storm-struck tree. 'Are you determined to kill us all? Do you really have no idea how to live?'

'No.' Daimonia frowned. 'How should I live?'

'STOP TRYING TO CHANGE EVERYTHING!' he shouted in her face.

'I'm not!' Her fingers drifted through her face and hair, making warpaint of the mud.

'Are you going to be there when I get home to my wife? Are you going to tell her?' Purtur's hands twisted as if wringing Daimonia's neck. 'Are you going to tell her that Hem is dead?'

'It wasn't me who killed–'

'And as for what they'll do to Goodkin now. Don't you look away, not for a moment! Every lash will be because of you!' His eyes narrowed, as mean as a rat's. 'I can promise you this; I'm not travelling another mile with either of you!'

Daimonia had already left Purtur behind. She pushed, slid and squeezed her way to the front of the crowd. The mob had gathered around a tall hurting post, the head of which was chiselled to resemble Prince Moranion's perfect face. The wooden likeness was very appealing to the eye, with strong symmetrical features and an expression that implied courage, fairness and kind humour. Beneath the royal face the post was thick with red and brown stains.

Goodkin was marched into the shadow of the wooden prince. The militants tried to yank him around, but he retained his firm posture. Instead they made a great show of removing the Way Knight's mail, stripping him of all armour and clothes, intending to humiliate the fighter. The act revealed a formidable body brandishing muscles embattled from years of martial living.

The militants compared themselves unfavourably with the Way Knight's disciplined shape; even unarmed and naked he seemed to overpower them. In their contempt they struck and spat at him, but succeeded only in further exaggerating their relative impotence.

Daimonia looked at him anew; the truculent knight robbed of all his protection. His steady presence held the mob enthralled; no doubt any one of them would have wept and begged had they shared his fate.

However, the Way Knight's nonchalance provoked resentment from many observers. The crowd was growing substantially and Daimonia was alarmed to see how their sympathies had transformed. During Goodkin's fight with the militants, every man watching had wanted to be him, taking vicarious pleasure in his savagery. Now those same men wanted to see Goodkin punished and humiliated. A belligerent anticipation gleamed in their callous stares, like animals waiting to be fed.

An especially rosy-faced drunk swayed next to Daimonia. His eyes were stupid with ale, gleaming with a delirious ignorance that Daimonia felt furious to observe. As Goodkin was shackled to the post, the drunkard smiled and cheered. When the flesh-splitting whip got to work on Goodkin's back, the drunk laughed and made the sign of buggery with his fingers.

Daimonia's hand found the long handle of her dagger. She closed her eyes and slowly caressed its smooth finish with her thumb. It dawned on her that the weapon was a dark and sacred thing. Forged in distant Viland, the dagger had been the ceremonial weapon of a Visoth warlord, until that owner had met Jhonan on a battlefield. Daimonia's grandfather had felt a strong affinity with the jagged blade, preferring it to a Dallish knife. In Daimonia's hand it was a sharp shard of power.

Anguish emanated from her stomach to the tips of her fingers. She looked only at the crowd, cringing at the joyous whoop that followed each resound of the whip. Daimonia realised that people would side with whoever was most dangerous in any situation. She swam in this thought, staring only at the drunkard's face, hating his arousal at Goodkin's grunts.

Her dagger was inside the man's belly. The blade had opened the drunkard up and the bawdy joy in his face was usurped by agony and horror. He fell silently and without spectacle; sinking into the turbulent crowd, he seemed to drown among them. Whoever he was, whatever experiences he might have had were trampled underfoot.

Daimonia had murdered him. She had killed him right here in the midst of everyone and not a single person had witnessed it. As strangely as a dream, she felt outside her own actions as she sheathed the blade and wiped her wet palms on her dress. Only one set of eyes were upon her, watching and judging what she had done. The pain in the Way Knight's stare was great and terrible.

The Duke's Hospitality

Geld Knight Conrad Ernst lay stoking his desires until his mind became a black miasma of lust.

The Duke of Knave had proved an adequate host. Conrad had been provided with dinner, a well-furnished room and the use of one of the duke's daughters. Sadly the girl was nothing to brag about and had been overused by previous visitors. Conrad set her to polishing his armour while he lay, energetically contemplating the duke's wife.

At dinner he had been drawn to Lady Knave, so elegant, so knowing. Conrad had barely acknowledged the boring duke at all, preferring to idle his attention in the jewelled eye winking between Lady Knave's breasts. How she reminded him of the capable Elena-Beleka.

Geld business had been conducted satisfactorily. The tax ledgers were in order and riders were sent to Kraljevic to announce Sir Conrad's victory over the notorious John Grobian. This was a lie that Conrad had started to believe was true. He could vividly recall the battle he had never fought.

The Geld enforcers were scouting the streets of Knave for the, apparently terrifying, Way Knight who might claim otherwise. 'Find this rough Way Knight,' Conrad had urged them. 'Ensure he doesn't claim my glory.'

'Knave is a busy place,' Fotter had challenged. 'There might be half a dozen Way Knights here. How will we know the one?'

'Most Way Knights are second or third sons trying to scrape a living with no inheritance,' Conrad said. 'But we're not looking for some foppish noble. This Goodkin will be a well-travelled veteran, a true warrior of the road.'

Conrad sighed and let go of himself. The bed was uncomfortable and reminded him only of how much more generous the duke might have been. He pulled on a long nightgown and noticed the duke's daughter, who knelt polishing his steel codpiece. 'I want to be able to see my own face in it,' the Geld Knight encouraged her.

He arose and took the door handle in his sweaty palm, opening the way with the merest creak. The cool dark corridor was adorned with paintings of the duke's ancestors and Conrad tentatively crept past their accusing stares. His mind boiled with stimulation, anticipating the heady mix of lips and lace, of perfume, thighs and tresses of chestnut hair.

How long had it been since Conrad had seen a woman he had truly desired? There had been the innocent Vornir girl. Almost a pity to think of her now, burned to death with her grandfather. But the debacle at Jaromir brought back painful memories threatening to shrink his enthusiasm.

Conrad took the stairs and tried to sniff out Lady Knave's bedroom. Each floorboard contrived to creak noisily under his weight, announcing him like a robber. 'Please,' Conrad invoked the Secret God. 'Lead me to your pleasure.'

Something detached from the wall and moved swiftly towards him.

Conrad froze, caught between lust and fear. The shape was the Duke of Knave, and by the murderous grimace on his face, he knew Conrad's intention.

'My lord.' Conrad bowed awkwardly.

'Do you think I don't know where you're going?' the duke challenged. 'I saw the looks you exchanged with Janina. A beautiful wife is a curse!'

Conrad tried not to blink, blush or swallow. The duke was an important man, a cousin to the prince. His enmity would be a political disaster.

'You mistake me.' Conrad forced his lips into a seductive grin. 'You mistake my intention.' He gently cupped the duke in his hand and felt the weight there. 'It is you I wish to serve, my lord.'

In the dreary morning Conrad wandered the gardens with the duke's daughter as his squire. She was attentive and kind, carrying all the Geld Knight's bags as he wandered.

'You've not complained once,' Conrad told her. 'I should keep you as an example to my enforcers.'

'If it pleases you, Sir Conrad.' She blushed. Despite a droopy eyelid and sullen features, she was at least strong and obedient. 'No man has been as kind to me as you.' She had a simple goodness that was almost sinister.

It occurred to Conrad that the girl was doting on him. A thousand ways to hurt her swam through his mind, but wasn't he evolving beyond such petty amusements?

'What do you see?' he asked her with genuine curiosity. 'What do you see when you look at me?'

'I see Chrestos Lightbringer,' she declared without hesitation. 'I see a god.'

Conrad was astounded. He felt a burning in his bosom; the girl had seen the divinity within. He took her jaw in his hand and lifted her face. 'What is your name?' he asked with a sudden grandness to his manner.

'Dobra,' she answered. Her voice was short of breath. 'Dobra Knave.'

'You will be my first disciple,' he told her solemnly, placing a chaste kiss on her forehead.

'Sir Conrad!' An infuriating voice interrupted the sacred exchange.

'What is it, Cain? Calm yourself.'

'I ran here.' The huge brawler leaned on his knees, catching his breath. 'We found the Way Knight. And you won't believe who he's with.'

The Enforcers

'We don't have to leave yet,' Daimonia argued. 'You need time to recover. You can't even wear your armour!'

'I will get you to Khorgov,' the Way Knight determined. 'You won't defeat me.'

'Defeat you?' Daimonia froze. 'I don't understand?'

'You've provoked vicious criminals. You've insulted Seidhr workers and interfered with militants in their duties. You've strayed from every rule of travel. But you won't defeat me, Daimonia Vornir. I will get you to Khorgov, even if it kills me.'

'There's really no need to take that tone—'

'So short a journey and just the two of us to make it. You won't break me before we get there.'

'This is very perplexing!' Daimonia helped the Way Knight down the tavern steps. A series of black archways lined the streets, portals to nowhere. 'I was beginning to warm to you, Goodkin. But I'm not sure what to make of this outburst.'

'Won't break me,' Goodkin muttered. 'I'll see my duty done.'

They continued in silence through the drizzly streets of Knave, looking like a pair of shabby outlaws. Goodkin wore a loose tunic and his tabard over his ravaged torso. His broadsword was sheathed on his hip and he held his worn shield loosely. Beside him, Daimonia stepped lightly through the puddled streets. Her dress was a crusty ruin adorned with muddy stains.

A meagre rain spat upon the rooftops as the militia changed shift and traders set out their pitches. Birds departed the looming towers, flocking to better fortune elsewhere. Daimonia mused that the gloomy morning was the perfect epilogue to the evening before.

Throughout the night she had tended Goodkin's wounds, cleaning the brutal cuts across his back. He had resisted, of course, but in the still room she had tended him by candlelight. 'Why choose this life?' she had whispered in the darkness. The prying question had died unanswered.

At breakfast, Purtur had met them with a bitter face. 'Like I told the girl, I ain't going another step with either of you.' Dark bags hung beneath his eyes, adding years to his face. 'It was ill fortune that brought us together.' When the Way Knight offered no reply, Purtur grew angry. 'Worst silver I ever spent!' He overturned the table as he left.

At the stables the groom was whistling cheerfully, hands shoved into his pockets. Seeing Goodkin and Daimonia, the groom waved and adjusted his cap. He led the couple across the courtyard, where stable boys mucked out stalls and travellers prepared for departure. Goodkin's and Daimonia's horses were together, each looking at the other uncertainly.

Daimonia was distracted by a fidgeting figure who was watching them with narrow eyes. He was a lean man with long greasy hair and a slick moustache. Their eyes met and the figure began to stroll over. His grin revealed two oversized teeth, like a rabbit's.

'She's done some miles,' the man told the Way Knight with a wink.

Goodkin protectively stepped in front of Daimonia.

'Talking about your palfrey.' The stranger nodded towards the horses, but his eyes were on the girl. 'Wouldn't mind a go on her myself.'

'I know you,' Daimonia said. 'You're a Geld enforcer.'

He made a small bow. 'Fotter's the name, trapping's the game!'

'You're in my way,' Goodkin told him.

A sneering youth swaggered up to join them, thumbing the pommel of his sword. Fotter seemed emboldened, moving closer. 'Scorcher and I are here for Miss Vornir. She owes Sir Conrad a debt.'

'What debt?' Daimonia's brows curled with irritation. 'Surely you haven't forgotten how my grandfather answered the Geld Knight's claim.'

'Sir Conrad is on his way right now. He is very keen to see you both.'

'No time.' Goodkin shook his head and turned away. 'I've been paid to take the girl to Khorgov.'

Fotter patted Goodkin's shoulder with a conciliatory smile. 'There's been a change of plan.'

Goodkin's shield exploded into Fotter's face. The trapper tumbled back drunkenly, clutching his nose as blood soaked his moustache. Goodkin grabbed a fistful of Fotter's straggly hair and dragged him about, pounding him barbarically.

'Geh the fuh off!' Fotter spluttered as his teeth cracked.

In a flash young Scorcher drew his sword and leapt at the Way Knight. The boy's attack was a graceful slice delivered with a flourish. Goodkin grabbed the boy's cloak and slung him into a pile of horse dung, where he slid and slipped over.

'Over here!' Fotter began shouting between gasps. 'They're over here!'

Hoods were thrown back and brawny figures emerged, a gang of men-at-arms revealed from hiding places in the courtyard. These were worthless blackguards and mercenaries scraped up from Knave's underbelly. These degenerate killers brandished weapons as mean as their faces; there were hooks and hammers, crude clubs and sharpened axes.

'Go!' Goodkin shoved the girl toward the horses.

Daimonia's heart fell through ice. Had these savages followed her all the way from Jaromir? She pictured the Geld Knight dragging himself ingloriously from the mud after her grandfather's triumph. She should have seen it then in Conrad's rancorous stare; he would be an implacable enemy.

Now she would die in this courtyard, brutalised by these weapons and the men wielding them. Her body became a thing awkward to control, her courage withering and flying away like an old leaf.

'Kill that scar-faced bastard!' Fotter was yelling with one finger lodged up his gushing nose.

Goodkin charged at the mercenaries, a war cry welling up from his throat. His opponents were disorganised, undisciplined and cared nothing for the men at their side. They faltered at the Way Knight's fearless advance. He shrugged off a mallet strike and capsized the first man who tried to grab him. They came at him in twos or threes as he blocked, slashed and slaughtered.

Fotter reached out to Daimonia. 'Come here, little bird,' he coaxed.

Daimonia began edging backwards towards her horse, unsheathing her Visoth war blade as she retreated.

'Silly little bird,' he cautioned. 'There's no need for that!'

Daimonia saw the apprehension in his face and decided they wanted her alive. She feigned a lunge and Fotter flinched like a coward, making an awkward shape with his arms and legs. Before the trapper could recover, Daimonia snatched his sabre from its scabbard.

'Give that back right now!' he scolded.

Daimonia advanced with both sabre and dagger, hatred arousing her senses. She jabbed and stabbed at Fotter, chasing him as he tried to dance away. A chance strike went straight through his palm, splitting the flesh and muscle. He whined terribly and stuck his bleeding hand under his armpit.

'Dirty chit!' Fotter snarled.

Daimonia decided to kill him. She tried to scissor his head off, but he ducked away with a petrified shriek. Daimonia persisted, snapping at him again with the blades, but succeeded only in puncturing his throat. Fotter began the work of dying with extreme reluctance, screeching and shaking around the stables.

'Ride!' Goodkin bellowed as he fought. His enemies closed and withdrew like a dragging tide. One advanced to strike while others sought openings as Goodkin defended. Stepping over the falling bodies of their allies, they gradually forced him back.

Young Scorcher had cast aside his reeking cloak. He raced to catch Daimonia, but she was already freeing her horse from its stall. He jabbed at the animal's face to drive it back.

'Bastard!' Daimonia yelled. Rage burned inside her, stretching its fiery wings, making her feel huge and powerful. She fought like a mummer's dance: a jab with the dagger, a slash with the sabre, a spin and stab. The blades tinged and twisted, finding their way through Scorcher's guard to pierce his chest.

'What?' Scorcher's fingers went to his reddening shirt. His head was tilted in confusion, amazed at his own mortality.

Daimonia mounted and rode as if spurring the horse with her will. She hurtled through the courtyard, knocking a vomiting warrior aside in her escape. Her heart and the horse were one, fleeing for precious life. All that was at stake drove her: the hope of her mother's love, the vengeance due her dead brother, the punishments she wanted to inflict. But even these passions were secondary to the need to survive.

The wind became precious, even the rain was a luxury long undervalued. The sensation of limbs and life was more priceless than the finest silks. She had barely begun to live, to experience life beyond the boundaries of her birth.

Passing unfamiliar buildings, Daimonia realised she was clear of danger. The panic was almost immediately superseded by euphoria; she had escaped, she would live.

She slowed the horse by a bridge, taking time to regain her breathing. Passing townsfolk gave her a wide berth – the wild girl mounted on a great steed. Daimonia didn't care about their disdainful glares; they knew nothing about her story. She was mere days from Khorgov, close enough to imagine bathing in maternal love. She could make the last leg of the journey alone, without the Way Knight's grim company.

Thoughts of Goodkin troubled her mind. He alone had understood the territory and what was required to traverse it. Time and again he had given of himself to protect her. But the Way Knight had frustrated Daimonia with his adherence to duty, his disinterest in fighting evil if it lurked the least bit off his path. Nothing had stirred him from servant to champion. Nothing except her.

The Geld Knight Conrad Ernst rode into the courtyard, announced by a regal anthem. He wore a look of special purpose; his fair eyebrows raised high with importance. The music summoned the attention of the combatants, the cowering stable hands and even the dying. Beside Sir Conrad, his disciple Dobra Knave blew gustily into a trumpet, her belly round with air. They were accompanied by two of the duke's finest cavaliers riding proud white stallions. The hulking enforcer Cain trailed behind, weighing down an old nag.

An aroused smile brightened Conrad's features. He surveyed the many dead mercenaries, satisfied that they had died instead of him. With some pleasure he noticed that Fotter had choked to death on his own blood. *I wished it and it was so*, Conrad reflected.

The great and terrible Way Knight was close to death. The man wore no armour, aside from a battered shield, and was barely standing. The few surviving mercenaries edged carefully around the tortured knight with ridiculous caution. Clearly the fight was over.

'Where's the girl?' Conrad asked Scorcher. The youth was the colour of chalk, leaning against the gate in his blood-saturated shirt.

'Escaped,' Scorcher replied breathlessly. 'She killed Fotter and then—'

Conrad strapped the boy across the face with his horse whip. It made such a satisfying impression that he did it again. The boy yelled and fell back weeping.

'Stop!' Conrad commanded the mercenaries. He caught the nasal sound in his voice again, but this time he didn't care. He was completely in control; life and death would be subject to his instructions.

The Way Knight was on one knee, staring up at him defiantly. His sword was thick with blood, as was his ragged tunic. Conrad noticed that the man was extremely harsh to look upon, adding to the impression of a formidable and implacable fighter.

'Get him up,' Sir Conrad instructed. It was unnecessary; the Way Knight was already rising, waiting for the inevitable.

Conrad dismounted and walked a full circle around the injured Way Knight, giving the wounded warrior time to behold his resplendent armour and bearing. 'I don't have a speech prepared,' Conrad said, 'and you look like a man who has seen the world as it truly is. Suffice to say, we are two men at cross purposes.' Conrad met the Way Knight's gaze full on. 'It is imperative you tell me Miss Vornir's whereabouts. Where she is going, what her intentions are and so forth.'

'Won't break me,' Goodkin grunted, more to himself than to Conrad.

'You' – Conrad pointed – 'tell me' – he imitated a talking mouth with his hand – 'where the girl is.' He made the sign of a whore with his lips and fingers.

The Way Knight stared blankly and then spat a thick glob of blood onto the ground.

'Cain, can you help our friend find his tongue?'

Cain lumbered up to the Way Knight and the two burly figures locked eyes. Cain was a good head taller and a great deal meatier. He rocked Goodkin's head with a punch that split the scarred skin in two.

Goodkin faced the ground, watching his blood spill upon the earth. An odd flap of skin dangled from beneath his nose, revealing his teeth and gums to ghastly effect. The enforcers jeered and laughed.

'Again,' Conrad ordered.

The next hit sent Goodkin sprawling across the ground, his sword spinning away from him. He crawled to retrieve it.

'No, let him,' Conrad declared when the mercenaries went to intervene. He watched the derelict figure grab his weapon and resume a fighting stance. Conrad recognised the opportunity to redeem his reputation.

'Come on,' the Way Knight goaded insolently.

Conrad unsheathed his sword with a look of holy majesty. He held it before his face, observing his own faultless reflection before focusing on his enemy. He glanced at the men who were watching, awaiting the contest between the two rival knights. He ran over and, with a yell of triumph, drove his sword at Goodkin's throat.

The Way Knight deflected the attack so violently that Conrad was face-slapped by the flat of his own blade. Embarrassed and smarting with pain, Conrad back-stepped quickly. Blinking copious tears, he wiped his seeping eye and glanced at the observers. His men believed in him, he could see it in their zealous stares. The only doubt he had to overcome was his own.

The Way Knight was drawing his strength, preparing for Conrad's next attack. He raised his sword above his head, tip down in a ready stance.

Sir Conrad dabbed his face with a kerchief and tossed it aside. He inhaled and then launched a flurry of quick strikes. Goodkin met each swing with strident counter-strikes, barely meeting Conrad's speed but more than matching his strength. Their fight circled through the courtyard, the warring steel clashing as they duelled.

Conrad kicked a slop bucket into the air, hooking it with his boot. The spinning bucket met Goodkin's shield and was batted back. Conrad wailed as he was showered with excrement. Sopping with waste, he retreated towards his men. Was this the secret baptism he had been awaiting?

'Just kill him.' Conrad buried his face in his elbow. 'Just bloody kill him!'

Daimonia's horse burst into the courtyard, as fierce and fleet as lightning. She rode into Sir Conrad, sending him flying like a thrown doll. His agonising shrieks were the worst she had ever heard.

'Hurry!' she screamed at Goodkin. The Way Knight ran awkwardly towards his horse as Daimonia rode among the wounded, hacking and stabbing from her saddle.

'Don't let them escape!' Dobra Knave blared at the duke's men. The cavaliers immediately obeyed, spurring their horses to give chase. Conrad rolled on his back, crying.

Daimonia and Goodkin goaded their mounts to flee the courtyard with abandon, leaving behind a chorus of curses and screams. They ploughed recklessly through streets and gardens, overturning market stalls and flattening patrolling militants. This time Daimonia's elation was a sword of searing fire; she had become the protector.

As they raced through the eastern gate, the duke's cavaliers were still in determined pursuit. These adept riders were talented horsemen and would not be easily evaded. Their plumed helms bobbed in the breeze as they chased their prey.

Immediately outside of Knave, a meandering train of wagons approached. At the forefront rode an illustrious noble from House Guldslag. This wealthy dignitary was perched joyfully upon an extravagantly coated camel. He was escorted by a regiment of Guldslag soldiers marching uniformly behind him.

Passing at speed, Goodkin swung his fist into the noble's mouth. He knocked the man clear off his panicked camel and into the astonished men below. The resulting confusion of spears, horses, men and livestock made a devastating trap for the pursuing cavaliers, who rode headlong into the turmoil.

'We're free,' Daimonia breathed. 'We did it.'

Goodkin made no reply but instead nodded. He looked like a thing just born, wrinkled and bloody.

The forest called to them, offering safety in its many pockets of darkness. As they made for the trees, a single Geld enforcer escaped from the carnage and rode furiously in pursuit. He was a strapping Afreyan warrior gripping a keen-edged ebony scimitar.

'Don't stop,' Goodkin yelled. The Way Knight veered his horse around to engage the Afreyan, straining to raise his sword as he moved into a mounted charge.

They exchanged blows as the horses drew together, a mad savagery gripping them both. The Afreyan lost a finger in the clash, but had the mettle to stand in his stirrups and retaliate. The strike was so hard the Way Knight's sword broke, and the scimitar sank into his flesh. Goodkin buckled in his saddle, leaking blood into the wind.

Daimonia slowed to witness the scene, her heart thundering as she watched Goodkin trying to ride away from the enforcer. The Afreyan was kicking his horse madly, delirious with the prospect of the kill. The horses raced towards her.

A terrible foreboding gripped Daimonia and her eyes welled with tears. She reached for her bow and nocked a single trembling arrow. Goodkin was bleeding to death and the Afreyan was riding up, teeth clenched, to hack him to pieces. As the horses rode wildly, Daimonia tried to still her feelings, to lose herself in the arrowhead.

With a breath she let loose a shot aimed at the large target of the Afreyan's horse. The arrow lacerated the animal's forehead crudely. The creature faltered in distress and Daimonia laughed as horse and rider were both dashed upon the ground in a neck-breaking collision.

'Good shot.' Goodkin nodded as he caught up with her.

They pushed on into the woods, Goodkin pressing hard against his gushing wound. He was trembling, uttering something, but it was beyond comprehension.

'Don't worry,' Daimonia told the knight. 'I won't leave you.'

A Single Silver Piece

They raced determinedly over rippling brooks and beneath the far-reaching arms of monumental trees. An eruption of perfect flowers spread around them in a vast train of flourishing beauty. As the Way Knight began to choke and fail, they rode into a great and ominous shadow.

Goodkin groaned and fell from his horse, landing violently amid the treasury of colour. Daimonia descended and landed by the Way Knight's side.

Luscious fragrances welcomed the girl as she knelt in the primitive grandeur. Her fingers caressed the man's hard face. The coarse skin was rough to her delicate touch, each scar containing a soft valley amid the rifts of ruined flesh.

Goodkin's eyes returned her stare like hard stones. 'I am done,' he told her.

'No,' Daimonia answered. She wondered whether it was wrong to feel powerful at this moment. She felt like a character in a strange tapestry, surrounded by colour as she knelt by her dying companion.

An imposing carving of Mother Cerenox towered over the grove, crowned by the foliage above. The wooden Goddess was tall and substantial, shaped from a standing tree. For eyes she had two deep alcoves wherein were set a cluster of unlit candles. Her belly was round with impending life.

'Great Mother,' Daimonia implored, 'please hear your daughter's prayer. I have sought you through the thunder and the rain. I have looked for you in the morning and in the night. I have stood on the precipice of death and yet not turned aside. Through it all this man has been my shield, my brother and my protector. Let him stay awhile longer before taking him in your arms, for I cannot find you alone.'

The Great Mother was silent.

Daimonia beat her fist against the wood, her eyes alight with fervour. 'Hear me!' she cried.

A single butterfly broke loose from atop the Goddess and fluttered to an unsightly cave in the worst darkness of the grove. Daimonia followed, rushing through the long grass. At the edge of the cave she paused and stared into the gloom. It was silent. Cautiously she leaned against the timeless stone and took a single step into the blackness. She immediately recoiled as her fingers slipped amid a sticky mass of mucous and meat. Disgusted, she discovered hundreds of snails clustered amid an elaborate maze of slime.

Wiping her fingers against her dress, Daimonia yelled into the cave, 'Is someone there? Please help me!'

A deep croaking sound erupted from the dim hollow. A figure began to drag itself up, wheezing as it climbed. A raw unearthed scent pervaded the air. Daimonia took a step back, poised to flee.

An elderly woman emerged, clad in shabby skins and leaning on her knees to climb. She was so long in years that every part of her face was

175

crevassed with deep lines of age. Her yellowed eyes peered in two directions simultaneously, one of them set fiercely on Daimonia.

'Mind the snails!' the old woman howled.

'My friend is dying!'

'So is mine!' the crone snapped. With wrinkled fingers she plucked a broken-shelled snail from the wall and stroked its moist body. 'Go to the Great Mother, little one,' the woman prayed, making a tomb of her gnarled hands.

'There is a man dying over there!' Daimonia shrieked in exasperation.

'Is he more special to the Goddess than this one?' the crone rasped, her spittle filling the space between them. 'This precious one you've killed in your carelessness?'

'Yes! I think so. No...I don't know,' Daimonia admitted.

'Who are you?' The crone's dominant eye scrutinised Daimonia. 'What do you want?'

'I am no one.'

'A satisfactory introduction,' the crone decided with a sigh. 'I am Sister Tulanae, a delightsome holy virgin in the service of the Goddess.' Her lips creased into a saggy smile. 'I know, I know. It seems hard to believe I have kept myself pure all these years and it's not as if I didn't have suitors–'

Daimonia's hand lashed out and slapped the old face. 'Help us!' she demanded, her lips curling with rage.

'How dare you!' The crone rose up like a great owl, empowered by wisdom and age. Her sleeves became baggy wings and her long nailed fingers tensed like talons. With a huge inhalation she filled her belly and

176

then blew words into the wind with impassioned deliberation. 'IN THE NAME OF MOTHER CERENOX I REBUKE YOU AND FORBID YOU FROM LAYING A HAND UPON ME!'

Daimonia slapped the leathery old face again. 'Help us!' she insisted.

Sister Tulanae visibly diminished. 'Young people have no respect,' she whined, curling up around herself. When she had rubbed the soreness from her face, she dared to look up again. 'Very well, let's see to your friend. There's an altar below, sanctified to the Great Mother. Help me get him to it.'

Goodkin was dragged groaning into the cave, where old candles melted in coarse alcoves and odd malformed things lurked in jars. Sister Tulanae insisted on administering to the knight alone. Daimonia reluctantly backed out of the hole, careful not to bash the snails as she left.

In the grove Daimonia found her way back to the comfort of the Goddess. Beneath the maternal figure's shelter, she allowed fatigue to finally take her. She fell to the flower bed, as if to her own death.

Leaves gambolled around the grove, stirred by a sinister wind. Darkness snuck from hollow and nook, tentatively at first but then with growing boldness until the shadows became a crawling smoke invading the sweet pasture.

Daimonia was unable to move or blink. Fixed on her back, she stared up at the encroaching night. Her thoughts became tired and dreadful, full of cosmic catastrophes and unpleasant mythology, the end of all things in a hail of screaming stars. Staring at the vastness of space,

Daimonia felt the world had been turned upside down and feared she might fall into the never-ending darkness. She gripped the plants to save from flying from the earth, her muscles straining against the irrepressible pull.

A distant winking star sailed towards her, launching from its place in the heavens. Daimonia's eyes were wide with wonder as the brilliance of the star expanded, casting a silver luminescence over the great forest. The whole grove groaned in anticipation of an incomparable event or manifestation. In the centre of the light, Daimonia discerned a single golden figure.

Daimonia awoke with a gasp. The world seemed to spin and a great oneness filled her heart, as if she were indistinguishable from the flowers or the stream. The dawn sun warmed her with its watchful light.

Sister Tulanae sat nearby, poking the last embers of a log fire with her staff. She stared at Daimonia as if expecting her to give birth to an idea.

'I had a dream,' Daimonia said.

'Tell me.'

'A man came to me from the sky. A superior figure cloaked in fire.'

'You dreamed of Chrestos.'

'The brother of the Goddess?' Daimonia wondered.

'Yes and no,' Tulanae replied. 'Chrestos is not one man, but that which is best in all men. Be they son or father, friend or lover.'

Daimonia shuddered involuntarily. 'What is the meaning of such a dream?'

'Such a visitation is very portentous. It means you've been anointed as one of us. You're a daughter of the Goddess, one of the sisterhood.'

'No,' Daimonia asserted. 'I do not plan to spend my life watching shadows in a cave.'

'Then how will you spend your years?' Sister Tulanae asked with a crafty smile.

'As I am. As Daimonia.'

This provoked a hearty laugh from the crone. 'How could you be anything else?'

Daimonia stood. Her body was wet with sweat and her cheeks were red as apples. 'Will Goodkin live?'

'No.' The crone flinched. 'He has joined the stars above. There he will wait until the end times, when they fall and take us all.'

Daimonia ran from the crone, the animals scurrying from her path. She paused by the cave, stopped by a terrible stench. Then with trepidation she entered, as if into the mouth of a dead animal.

The Way Knight lay naked on the altar, like a relief in stone. Daimonia approached with quiet reverence. She forced herself to look at Goodkin's face; it seemed easier now the man was gone. But she could see no scars, only dignity and perseverance.

Daimonia's head found his chest, listening for a heartbeat. When no sound came, she lingered, resting her face and arms on his cold body. The vast silence spoke for her loss.

'All journeys must eventually be made alone.' Sister Tulanae hobbled into the cave.

Daimonia wiped her eyes and sat up. She noticed that Goodkin's palm was open, offering a single silver denarius on a chain. *For me?* Daimonia wondered.

'There, there,' the crone encouraged. 'Death belongs to us all. We only weep when it gets someone else first!'

'Can you speak the Way Knight's last words as the adjurators do?'

Sister Tulanae laughed derisively.

Daimonia scowled and gently unhooked the chain from Goodkin's hands. She hung it around her own neck, rubbing the coin softly between her fingers.

'A Way Knight symbol.' Sister Tulanae raised a grey eyebrow. 'The sign of warriors and hardy travellers. Who are you hoping to fool with that?'

'Myself.'

Tulanae presented Daimonia with the Way Knight's folded tabard. 'Fare well on your journey,' she encouraged.

They left the cave in silence and walked the grove under the watchful eyes of the Goddess. Daimonia untied Goodkin's horse and let it go, although it merely cantered around the grove. Her own mount was impatient to leave. The lonely task of reaching Khorgov rolled out in her mind.

'Sister.' Daimonia's voice was imploring. 'Give me the flaming sword of the Goddess.'

'It is lit already, in your heart.'

At the forest's edge Daimonia emerged, leading her horse by her side. Her hair was alive with wave after wave of voracious wind. She looked to the vast clouds shadowing the plains between Knave and Khorgov. The vista was huge, full of possibility and potential danger. In the distance she spied travellers heading to and from surrounding villages and hamlets. Their distant faces appeared small and scared on their journey, hopeful for a protector.

Daimonia turned determinedly toward Khorgov and readied herself for the final run. In one fist she held Goodkin's worn tabard and on a whim she pulled the garment over her clothes. The bloodstained fabric rippled in the wind, like a raised sail.

Musical Interlude

The Geld Knight Conrad Ernst briskly cleaned John Grobian's severed head in a wooden bucket. So much of the giant face was missing that water leaked from a multitude of cracks and holes. Painstakingly Conrad used an old knife to pick grime from the ruined teeth, but when the first one popped out, he gave up that effort.

'Grobian, please,' Conrad admonished. 'You must look your best when presented to the prince!'

The head did not reply and Conrad sniffed it suspiciously. It was going to be a long journey to Kraljevic with this rancid companion.

'Maybe a little perfume, my lord?' Dobra Knave gathered her skirts and strode across the tavern bedroom to her master. 'Either under your nose or a little on the outlaw's head.'

Conrad rewarded the girl with a mild smile. How useful she was becoming. He had firmly refused when the Duke of Knave had tried to offer her services to another guest.

'That won't be possible,' Conrad had informed the duke.

'Not possible!' The duke's old veins had almost exploded.

'Dobra is an agent of the Geld now. She won't be entertaining any more of your guests.'

'Fine.' The duke had flared his nostrils bitterly. 'Take the useless

182

whore. I'm tired of seeing her miserable face anyway.'

'Very good, my lord.' Conrad didn't bother to bow before departing.

They had left Knave, laughing at their own scandalous behaviour.

That night Conrad had been in too much pain to sleep. Dobra had brewed hemlock, henbane and wine. Once he had drunk himself unconscious, she had tended his wounds, cleaning and wrapping them like a surgeon.

As they rested in the Wayfarer's Tavern, the Geld Knight mused that Daimonia Vornir would almost certainly have escaped to Khorgov. Conrad wondered whether it would be petty to chase her there. A far better prize awaited him at Kraljevic; the outlaw's head might even earn him initiation in the fraternal Order of Saints.

Dobra sat by an open window and began to pluck a small harp. Beneath her frilled sleeves, her hands danced along the strings, teasing out a pleasant sound.

'Please don't,' Conrad moaned. He had no desire to indulge the vapid hobbies of bored girls.

Smiling away Conrad's grumpiness, Dobra simply continued, demonstrating great skill in her use of the instrument. The tune was like a guileless child, cautious at first yet trusting in its steady progression. It gave voice to that which is silent: the solitude of a field, an unspoken feeling between friends, the longing between distant lovers. Ever more rousing the song became until it possessed the heart of a great poet.

So gentle was the melody, it seemed the girl's fingers played upon Conrad's soul. It was a song he had always known, but was hearing for the first time.

Inexplicably he began to weep. Hadn't he once known such joy and innocence? Hadn't there been a golden time before he was orphaned off to the Exalt Temple? Once he had a family, a delicate mother with eyes brimming with love. He could see her now, her face lit with joy as he snuggled beside her, golden curls adorning her divine face. The music drew him back into that safety and the simplicity of those lost childhood days.

He followed the memory through the farm he had played in as a boy. He saw his sister laughing and chased her through a maze of sunlit corn. Pushing through the crisp stalks, he was young and clean, unsullied by the world's corruption. Running through those fields again, he pursued an elusive question.

Who had that boy wished to become?

ACT THREE

THE GREAT MOTHER

Reunion

'Go no further!' a prophet warned. 'Turn back now! Nothing but tragedy awaits!' He stalked the road, unburdened by clothes, eminently comfortable with his gaunt and hairy body. All around him travellers shuffled past without as much as a glance. Horses brayed and pooed disinterestedly.

'The Goddess is generous in her anger!' the prophet insisted. His matted hair and shaggy beard gave him the wild authority of an ascetic. 'She both gives and receives wounds, each more grievous than the last. Her season will be enjoyed by crows!'

Only Daimonia watched the prophet perform among the accumulating travellers. She noticed his lively face and his determination to contort his body into a wild variety of expressions and shapes. He used gesture and intonation to elicit attention, but not a single person would meet his gaze. Even the horses focussed only on what lay ahead.

Khorgov was a maze of shade and darkness, a tenebrous city with no clear beginning or end. Refugees simply arrived at the expanding outskirts and sought to establish themselves on the spot, surrounding others who had done the same. In the far distance dark turrets, citadels and towers defined the boundaries between earth and sky, but they seemed an adventure away.

'Behold the terrible city,' the prophet insisted, clawing the sky with his hands. 'Go on,' he encouraged a child whose attention he had snagged. 'Really take a look at it.' The boy clung to his mother's skirts, preferring to explore his nose with his finger.

The prophet danced and flapped, expending enough energy to wake the dead. 'Behold the great mother,' he tried again. 'Her tits are dry and she is unable to give her children aught to succour them.' He reminded Daimonia of the narrator of a play, being both within and without the scene simultaneously.

'Go back!' he commanded Daimonia as their eyes met.

She was in the thick of the crowd, her blood-red tabard like a beacon to those who journeyed alongside. 'Why?' she replied, meeting his gaze with a frown. 'Do you see my fate?'

'Ah, go on with you.' He waved her past dismissively. 'Everyone thinks they are special.'

Daimonia rode slowly through the expanding urban fringe. Here homes had been made of whatever was at hand. Walls were mud and straw packed between wooden slats. Doors were merely blankets and skins. Fires burned everywhere and for every conceivable purpose.

She proceeded through the impoverished community, feeling shame at the relative wealth she had enjoyed at home. Undernourished babies sobbed, their cries competing with the bark of dogs. Waste poured from a collapsed dwelling, flooding the occupants who remained stubbornly within. Every human act occurred in the open, from childbirth to cremation.

Daimonia negotiated a path for some hours, refusing to buy some famous bones and trying not to ride down a gang of obstreperous chickens that blocked the way. She was surprised when she finally came upon stonemasonry and the edge of the city proper. The western gate was patrolled by scores of sour-faced militants garbed in grey-black tunics and feathered caps. They were haunted by the mocking caws of birds, who shat liberally over them and all over everybody attempting to enter or leave.

It was becoming dark as Daimonia advanced through the threshold, her heart burning with trepidation. Now that the moment was close, her mouth ran dry at the thought of informing her mother of Niklos' death. Would her mother scream and hurt herself? Would she blame Daimonia? What form would her mother's grief take before they could avenge the deed together?

She needed to be back in her own bed at Jaromir, but how very far away her home seemed now. The distance could be measured in corpses, the route traced by painful moments never to be forgotten. She longed for her small world, for her leaky room and for gruff old Jhonan. Most of all she wished that Goodkin were by her side, protecting and guiding her onwards. Without him she began to feel unshielded and weak.

Daimonia found herself beside a series of cages hung above the street. They were filled with bony, bearded men who stared hungrily at the people below. Daimonia drew alongside one such cage and stared wide-eyed at the occupant, who had made a tidy home of his incarceration.

188

The man had created curtains from his cloak, which were fastened to his cage with boot laces. His hood hung, thick with excrement, from beneath the cell. His finger and toenails were exceptionally long and thick with filth.

'Why are you here?' Daimonia asked.

The man looked genuinely surprised. He licked his sore-covered lips and leaned over towards the girl, pressing his nose through the cage and sniffing loudly.

'Get away from there!' someone shouted haughtily.

Daimonia turned to see an obese nobleman wearing resplendent robes of office. He promptly waddled up to the girl, a train of men chasing hurriedly after him, carrying food, books and cushions.

'Young woman,' the noble addressed her curtly, 'clearly you are a stranger here, or you would know that speaking to the Vendicatori implies sympathy with the rebellion.' He pointed to the wretched cages. 'If the militants see you, you'll end up with a cage of your own or locked away beneath the fortress.'

'Vendicatori?' Daimonia looked at again at the cramped prisoners. Were these ragged men the dangerous revolutionaries plotting to undermine the Accord? They didn't look like much of a threat, having been deprived of every dignity, their shame exhibited to the world.

'I'm no rebel,' she assured the noble. 'I seek my mother, Captain Catherine Vornir of the Knights of the Accord.'

'Captain Vornir is the castellan of Khorgov Fortress.' The noble pointed eastwards to where a mountainous structure loomed over the city like a dark glacier. 'She both serves and protects the Benevolent Council.'

'Well?' The squire crossed his arms. 'What is it?'

'I'm the daughter of Catherine Vornir,' Daimonia answered in the most polite voice she could muster. The fortress was a huge and confusing place, around which she'd wandered questioning unhelpful strangers before finding the castellan's squire.

'And I'm Prince Moranion,' he sneered.

'Is that so?' Daimonia's eyes flashed at the impertinent remark. 'It seems your majesty and beauty have been much exaggerated.'

'Har, har!' The squire chuckled with a show of grotty teeth. 'Very funny. Now be off with you.'

'I need to see my mother,' Daimonia pressed. 'I've come all the way from Jaromir.'

'I wouldn't know my own mother,' he replied, 'let alone yours.'

Daimonia bit the air. 'I've not come this far to be stopped by you. Let me in!'

'Calm down,' the squire surrendered. His eyes flicked over the girl's scowling face. 'I can see the resemblance well enough.'

Daimonia followed the man through chambers both busy and dark. A quivering prayer escaped her lips. 'Mother, I am finally here,' she whispered. The length of her journey tailed her, like the train of an extravagant dress.

190

They rose up a narrow staircase, taking three steps at a time. 'Here we go,' the squire said. They came to a small door embellished by feather-shaped hinges. 'This room is Captain Vornir's private quarters. I'll give her a shout for you if you like.'

Unable to hesitate, Daimonia opened the door, intruding upon a chamber of darkness. The air was hot with candle flame and the reek of human sweat. Within the warm cell, shadows wrestled and grunted.

'Mother,' Daimonia called softly into the dark. 'Mother, it's me.'

Daimonia thought she heard curses before a voluptuous figure uncoupled from the shadows and stepped towards the doorway. Candlelight revealed a familiar curve of cheek and chin, enough for Daimonia to be certain.

'Mother,' she exhaled, throwing herself into the dark shape and hugging with all her might. She squeezed the woman's flesh, her tears rolling onto the cool skin. Dry thirst found a point of boundless gratification. *This moment*, Daimonia rejoiced. *This moment forever.*

At first it seemed she held a corpse, so stiff was the reaction. Then very gradually a hand rose and placed itself on Daimonia's shoulder. It rested briefly before pushing the girl away.

'Why are you here?' the shadow asked.

Another figure emerged, a young man panting heavily as sweat shone on his body. His eyes met Daimonia's and then explored her figure with an appraising smile. 'Did she just call you mother?' he asked Catherine.

'Hush, Kasamir.' Catherine removed the young man's fingers from her thigh. 'Daimonia, I asked you a question.'

'Yes, sorry.' Daimonia wiped her eyes. 'It's just a bit overwhelming. I've come so far.'

'If Jhonan has died, then you're to live with Adjurator Ivan. It's been arranged.'

'Grandfather is alive,' Daimonia assured her mother. 'The first news I have for you is simply that I am here.'

'So I see,' Catherine replied. She looked to the squire, who was staring determinedly at the ground. 'It's late. Magpie will find you a room. Tomorrow you can tell me what this is all about.'

'I knew you'd be pleased.'

The door was closed and Daimonia realised she was trembling.

'Come along, girl.' Magpie beckoned. 'Best you sleep on this happy reunion. After all, the heart can only take so much.'

Glass

Morning found Daimonia peering from a high window, hair drifting in the smoky breeze. From the fortress she could glimpse the city's labyrinthine depths, the deep paths and passages where light faltered. Prosperity decreased from the centre out, from the decorated council mansions to the farthest shanties.

Daimonia leaned sleepily into the wind, allowing it to dry the tears on her cheeks. Last night's curt dismissal had scared her, kept her awake with doubts. Was she still the unlovable girl her mother needed to escape from? Perhaps she should be buried, like an unwanted doll in the earth.

She climbed onto the window ledge and sat, her long legs dangling over the drop. From this height she could fall and die twice over; it would be a splendidly violent death. She closed her eyes and rehearsed it, saw the moment when skin left stone and exhilarating free fall spun her.

Her skull would bite the earth and she would wash the whole city with blood.

Voices roused the girl from imagination and drew her attention to the sight of knights gathering on the bridge below. Clad in armour they stood, legs apart, shields slung on arms or backs. Their Accord tabards were grey with wear, blemished according to their years.

One veteran knight wore a tabard that was black with experience. He was regaling the others with a story that involved impersonating girls' voices and won a crescendo of laughter at the end.

Daimonia's mother strode out to join the men. Captain Catherine Vornir was a dark-browed woman with cropped hair and a short sharp nose. She wore a leather tunic armoured with hundreds of overlapping rings and a white woollen cloak. Seeing her again, Daimonia stopped breathing.

Each knight nodded or saluted as Catherine approached. She smiled at them as if they were her sons, gave instructions and watched as they proceeded to organise patrols of city militants.

Daimonia was aghast to realise that Catherine was leaving with them. 'Mother!' she shouted, leaning out as far as she dared. 'Mother, you've forgotten me!' But the knights were already marching their units purposefully across the bridge.

'Forgive me, brother,' she prayed. 'There is not enough love for the living, let alone the dead.'

Daimonia retraced the route by which Magpie had led her until she rediscovered her mother's room. This time she paused at the threshold,

194

placing one hand on the door as solemnly as if it were a tomb. *Is this a trespass?* Daimonia wondered. Biting her lip, she pushed open the door.

The room beyond was as silent as a temple, the shadows suggesting still figures in the dark. Daimonia crept inside, her fingers tickling the air like a thief's. She went first to the damp bed, where her mother had writhed with that man, the young lover who had invaded Daimonia with his eyes. She cringed at the recollection, wanting to shed her skin and scream. Instead she rent the sheets with her dagger, laughing with each rip. The Visoth steel came to life at her bidding, shredding fabric as it had once shred flesh.

When it was done, she began to examine everything, seeking some evidence of her mother's affection. *There must be something here of me,* Daimonia mused. *Something of our old life together.*

Her fingers ran along a shelf of books. Stories had given Daimonia pleasure when lonely. She had found solace in the troubles of heroes, loved their weaknesses more than their strengths. Lost in words, she had lived a dozen other lives, but those tales had little prepared her for real adversity and sorrow.

Fine gowns lay cast across a table, discarded carelessly. Weapons and armour lay everywhere, evidence of Catherine's determined crusade against the disobedient Vendicatori. Dead flowers hung limp in a jar.

Pillars of wax surrounded a small shrine, upon which stood a crude wooden effigy. The idol was a shoddy likeness of the Great Mother, a deformed representation of the Goddess. Beside it sat a birth-rite bell and a sheet of dusty glass.

As Daimonia approached, a wild figure rushed up to meet her. She saw a ferocious girl with wolfish hair, scarred lips and muddy cheeks. Her eyes were half-closed and appeared guarded and cunning, as if she had crawled through a battlefield to get here.

Daimonia wiped dust from the glass, wondering at the revelation. Was this the face her mother had been confronted with?

The knights returned as evening fell, their arrival made loud by drunken shouts.

Daimonia was in the dining hall, freshly bathed and wearing one of her mother's gowns. Petals had perfumed the water and their scent hung about her still. Her hair was freshly oiled and combed into glistening waves. All afternoon she had worked with Magpie to clean and prepare for the knights, before using her mother's bathtub and clothes.

'Service is its own reward, I suppose,' Magpie had reflected as he scraped shit from Sir Kasamir's boots.

'What kind of person is my mother?'

Magpie had leant up quickly with one hand on his crooked back. 'Well, the castellan has a great deal of responsibility,' he mused. 'Everyone here answers to her, excepting the Benevolent Council themselves. And she's one of those women – begging your pardon – with a will that won't bend one inch. So the whole fortress has to kind of bend itself around her.' He raised one eyebrow while lowering the other, making a lopsided expression.

'I wish I was like that.'

'It's a poor description,' he admitted. 'I'm a squire not a poet.'

The returning knights were less gallant than Daimonia hoped, treading muck into the hall and helping themselves to food without as much as a prayer. Daimonia moved among them, offering bread she had baked herself. Most grabbed a roll while slurping down soup, but one man took a fistful of the girl's backside in his hand.

'Daimonia!' Catherine Vornir's voice pierced the hall. She stood by the door, her chin high and eyes narrow.

Daimonia put down the food and ran to her mother. The gown clung comfortably to her body and her chest swelled with pride at how she had made herself pretty. Scars and bruises aside, she could pass for a noblewoman's daughter. Drawing close, she went to initiate a hug, but it became an awkward wave.

'You're going home,' Catherine informed her. 'It's been arranged.'

Daimonia's eyes widened to see a white-bearded Way Knight lurking in the porch. He was weighing a payment of silver, squeezing the coin pouch like a tit.

'I'm not leaving!' Daimonia clenched her fists.

'Yes, you are.' Catherine placed a gloved hand on her daughter's shoulder. Her grip was uncomfortably tight. 'You're not well.'

'Not well?' Daimonia pulled away.

'I know you can't see it.' Catherine smiled faintly.

'I don't understand what you mean.'

Catherine sighed and made the sign of prayer with her hands. 'You really don't remember, or are you just pretending? However much love I gave you, it was never enough. And when you couldn't get what you needed, you hurt me, Daimonia. The truth is you're dangerous and it's

197

not safe for me to be around you.' She reached for Daimonia's hair, caressing it with her fingers. 'Please understand; I have another life now. I'm not your mother anymore.'

Daimonia tried to scream, but the air had become elusive. Instead her cheeks became redder and redder until they were roasting on her face. Her mother's words became a series of incomprehensible noises such as an animal might make. 'I'm staying!' Daimonia finally screamed and when nothing happened she screamed again, her throat straining. Every eye in the hall was fixed on the impassioned youth, but no one was moved to intervene.

She saw it then. It lurked in the merest corner of her mother's otherwise concerned smile, but it was unmistakable. It was contempt.

Daimonia broke away. She fled through the doorway and down the plummeting steps to the bridge below. She descended into the city falling deeper and darker through shadow.

Skin

Khorgov never knew silence. Grunts and cries emerged from countless buildings. Screams and sobs were present in every dingy street. Intrusive voices made a dirge of the night as thousands of lives intertwined.

Adrift in the city, Daimonia searched for a quiet place to die. It was over. Her dream of reunion and revenge had been a fantasy. There was no heroic mother who would save her. There would never be any justice for her brother's death. There wasn't even an enemy to fight unless the indifference of the world could be called a foe.

Baron Leechfinger, Prettanike, the Geld Knight and even Catherine Vornir, they had been the sovereigns of her nightmare, the murmurers in the dark against whom she was powerless. But in truth they were nothing but shadows, echoes of a Secret God that worshipped itself.

Wandering through Khorgov's streets, Daimonia saw her own struggle reflected in the faces of strangers. It was in the canny gaze of the too-wise child and in the curled back of the menial worker. It was present in the prison cages and wrapped around the hurting posts. It all drew to the same inevitable conclusion: the Accord was a lie.

She sobbed, passing a gang of brightly robed boys lounging upon every conceivable surface. The young men wore looks of well-rehearsed meanness, offering beady-eyed stares to each stranger. She avoided a pathway where a patrol of grunting militants took turns punching and kicking someone's head.

Hours of misery passed before a rare and enticing sound caught the girl's attention. It was the ring of happy voices, laughter and applause. Hungrily she followed the strand of sound through the dark archways and canopied streets, longing to know its source.

A company of players were staging a lively theatrical drama, rousing their audience with feats of voice and posture. Their outlandish costumes made their roles immediately recognisable as characters from the cosmic myth. A smile warmed Daimonia's face as she recalled the acting troupe whose performance had delighted her at Jaromir.

The Khorgov players wore masks shaped in leering expressions. They were enacting a series of lewd situations and innuendos that reduced the story of the Goddess to a series of crude and violent encounters. Wandering in the labyrinth, Ceresoph was portrayed as a tempestuous youth beset by lecherous predators. The actors bent and thrust as the street audience clapped and chuckled. Daimonia felt her interest waning and pulled away in disgust.

On the opposite corner stood a stocky Urothian wearing a velvet cap, silver rings and a robe with fur-trimmed sleeves. He was smirking at Daimonia, rocking on his heels with his thumbs tucked into his belt.

Daimonia found the foreigner both strange and striking. The Urothian's cheekbones were extraordinarily pronounced and his jaw wide and square. Three exquisitely delicate women were pressed around him as if he were a prince. Their smiles and raised eyebrows appeared fixed in place.

The Urothian beckoned to Daimonia, calling her towards the colourful group. 'I think we are in terrible trouble,' he told her in his deep, dark accent.

'Are we?'

'If you insist on parading your beautiful hair around Khorgov, who will pay to look upon Astur's famous beauties?'

'They pay?' Daimonia began, but then sensing this was a flattery, she blinked with embarrassment.

'Such adorable eyes.' The Urothian laughed. He put his mouth to her ear. 'These streets are a bad place for a girl alone at night.'

'I have nowhere else to go,' Daimonia admitted. 'I have been cast out by my mother.'

'Come, little princess.' He grinned. 'Come into the safety of Astur's humble palace.'

Daimonia allowed Astur to lead her through the veiled archway and into the busy parlour beyond. The sweet-smelling hall was filled with silk drapes, wooden chests and armour painted to look like treasure. Turbaned musicians played a delirious melody, their pipe music masking primal sounds from the outer chambers.

Daimonia's heart thrilled at the charming attention, rich scents and entrancing sounds. 'This is lively company,' she found herself saying.

Astur laughed and led Daimonia through a thin candlelit corridor, teasing her with questions and compliments. He touched suggestively shaped ornaments and blew into them, making Daimonia laugh at the noises. Small figurines were everywhere, depicting little people and creatures.

'Do Urothians revere the Goddess?' Daimonia enquired.

Astur shrugged. 'We do not venerate the three-in-one Goddess. That story is just a cautionary tale for girls. In our culture we celebrate Rakasha, the spirit of all living things. Sex, birth and death – they are the fangs and horns of Rakasha.' He widened his eyes and showed his teeth, as if he himself were the deity.

Daimonia laughed again.

They came to an internal gate and Astur took a key from around his neck. Daimonia hesitated. 'What's through here?'

'For special guests,' Astur assured the girl with a firm hand on her back.

The lock clacked open and another Urothian greeted them on the other side. Daimonia found this man less pleasing than Astur. He was all belly and muscle, sweat dripping down his bald head.

'Who's this?' the new man grunted.

'Daimonia Vornir,' she replied defensively, emphasising her family name. She took a step backwards to find herself pressed against Astur's hard chest.

'That's a truly lovely name.' Astur's voice was warm and deep. 'What does it mean?'

'It's like flourishing, becoming – that kind of thing.'

'I see. Well, excuse us, Traegor. Miss Vornir and I are going to look at the paintings.'

Traegor let out a snort that fell somewhere between a cough and a laugh. He swaggered out of their way, revealing a set of stained steps beyond.

'I should probably go,' Daimonia decided.

'Nonsense.' Astur led her by the arm. 'I have something you won't believe.'

At the bottom of the steps a torchlit gallery shone in eye-catching colours. They stopped to admire paintings of sultans, palaces and fabulous creatures native only to Urothia.

'Is this real?' Daimonia stared at the foreign scenes, admiring a great cat in the plains.

'Very real,' Astur assured her, 'and as dangerous as it is beautiful. Just like a Visoth shield-maiden.' They had arrived at a small bedroom, where a fair-haired girl snored beneath an embroidered blanket.

'Dreja! Wake up!'

The girl's apple green eyes eased open sleepily. Her face was tired and puffy, half stuffed into a pillow. 'I'm tired,' she moaned.

'Please excuse Dreja.' Astur smiled, twisting an ornate ring on his finger. 'She works so very hard, but there's always more work to be done. Isn't that right, Dreja?'

Dreja drew herself up from the bedding, revealing a round and appealing face. Her cheeks were soft and rosy and her lips were shaped like a kiss. Shaking off a waking grumpiness, the girl stared quizzically at Daimonia.

'This is our new friend.' Astur placed a hand on Daimonia's shoulder. 'She's nowhere to go, but I've decided to take her under my wing.' His fingers caressed her black hair momentarily.

'Oh,' said Dreja.

'Perhaps a little spice to celebrate?' Astur took a pouch from his pocket, holding it close until Dreja tried to snatch it. He teased her back and forth, until he could steal a kiss. He bit the girl's lip lustily before allowing her to claim her prize.

Daimonia watched Astur bow and leave, unsure whether to follow. She turned to appraise the girl whose room she appeared to be sharing. Dreja's attention was entirely focussed on the pouch. Her body was athletic, even muscular, but her forearms were covered in a criss-cross pattern of scars.

'Who cut you?' Daimonia asked.

Dreja put her finger into the spice and licked it. She sat strangely, all legs and hair. 'I did,' she finally replied.

'Why?'

Dreja rolled her eyes. She looked Daimonia up and down, studying her gown with a look of displeasure. 'You shouldn't be here unless you have nowhere else to go.'

'I don't. And this doesn't seem like a bad place.'

'How can you be such a fool?' Dreja mocked. Her heavy Visoth accent lavished extra scorn on the question.

'I'm hardly a fool.' Daimonia's brows scored a dark line on her forehead. 'I can read and write. I can hunt and ride. And I've even killed. Does that sound foolish to you?'

Dreja stretched out her strong legs and yawned. Since waking, she had not been still for a moment. 'Do I seem impressed?'

'You shouldn't mock me. I'm a Vornir.'

'I don't know what that is.' Dreja shrugged. She grabbed a comb and began to draw it through her fine hair with a bored expression.

Daimonia's chest tightened with irritation. Her eyes studied Dreja's bright features with displeasure. 'My grandfather says too many Visoth are coming to Dalibor now. There will be no room for us Dallish.'

Dreja forced a laugh. 'Do you think we like being in your grey land? Who would choose this dreary place if they had any other choice?'

'Anyone would,' Daimonia answered. 'Our towns and cities are the best in the world.'

'Perhaps so, but remember that for every gain there is a loss.'

'Is that what passes for wisdom in Viland?' Daimonia hid a smile with her hand.

Dreja put down her comb and stood. 'Where I come from, the Baoth invaders kill the men and feed the children to their mothers. I do not think you know anything of the world beyond your soft Dallish life.'

Daimonia winced. Dreja was right, she knew little of the wider world, but she was not a stranger to horror. 'I don't have to prove anything to you.' She sulked. 'Sorrow isn't a competition.'

Dreja turned and grabbed the bag of spice, dipping her finger into the white dust. In a nearby room someone was crying.

Daimonia went to leave, but the door was bolted from without. She tried again as if force of will might make it open. When it didn't, she stood there for a long time, hovering between panic and surrender.

Finally she sighed and sat upon the bed. There were bloodstains on the sheets.

'Why would you turn a blade upon yourself?' she wondered aloud.

'Who else is there to hurt?'

'You should never let an enemy defeat you,' she encouraged.

Dreja examined the many scars that creased her arms. 'Thank you for the unwanted advice. But you should spend your energy escaping this place.'

'Why? I've just got here.'

'And you won't be staying for free.' Dreja raised glistening fingers from the pouch. 'Come,' she whispered, running her fingers over Daimonia's lips and gums. 'This will help.'

Tears welled before Daimonia's eyes like crystals. Her fingers and toes tingled, as if dipped into snow. She felt warm and whole, connected to everything, an ecstatic rush of intimacy and affirmation thrilling her.

But Dreja was squeezing her arm tightly, nails biting the skin. 'Forgive me!' she shrieked. 'You have to get out of here.'

Stone

Long before the sun could show its face, a slight figure limped through Khorgov's puddled streets. Barefoot, she shuffled, her wet gown stuck to her trembling body. The Visoth dagger glistened darkly in her hand.

Is this my blood? Daimonia wondered, lifting her arms like a dancer. She searched herself for wounds, finding her torso bruised but not pierced. A clump of hairy scalp lurked on one sleeve and she brushed it off abruptly.

How did I come to be here? Her memory was foggy, her stomach heaving. So invasive was the feeling that it seemed preferable to die than live another moment.

The night's events were disordered in her mind. She recalled numbness crawling up her arms and legs, her voice becoming slurred. She remembered uninhibited laughter bellowing from outside Dreja's room, the sound of men anticipating some pleasure. She had tried to rise but had fallen awkwardly by the foot of the bed.

They had grabbed her and she had fought back, unable to feel their blows. They had tried to hurt her and she had laughed at them, too numb to feel anything. And when she unsheathed her dagger, she had made them scream.

'Is this the worst you can do?' she asked the towering city. Her voice sounded like an old woman's, crackling and coarse. Khorgov's only reply was the ceaseless lament of voices.

The girl sank to her knees, retching by the side of a reeking cesspool. The sound echoed in the mouldering pit. Pulling her hair aside, she checked her teeth with her fingers, searching for new cracks or chips. Behind her something barked in the dark.

Daimonia turned to see a shadow striding towards her. The figure was bulky, hurrying forwards, hair a choppy mess. She crouched cautiously, ready to flee, but relaxed when she saw the man's eyes were crowded with friendly laughter lines.

'Oh dear.' The stranger took off his gloves and extended a hand. He was smiling, his cheeks round with kindness. 'What happened here?'

'Some men.' Daimonia sniffed. 'They thought they might force me.' She accepted the stranger's help and pulled herself upright. His hands were thick and strong like her grandfather's. She found his strength reassuring, although his breathing was hard and laboured.

'You poor thing,' the man consoled. 'Where'd you live?'

Daimonia opened her mouth to reply, but his hands were on her face, smothering her. She could taste the sweat and dirt on his palms, the tang of his unwashed skin.

'Now I don't mean to hurt you, really I don't,' he told her, pressing a blade to the side of her neck. 'But I need to feed my sons.' His hands searched her belt for a coin purse, and finding none, he grabbed her necklace. 'We have nothing, you see, and we all need to eat.'

Daimonia let out a cry of despair. Could an entire city be mad? Could a whole world? Fear was dead to her, but frustration and anger were giants. She reached for her dagger, but he snagged her wrist.

'What's this?' he said, pulling disgusting faces as if some creature writhed inside his brain. 'A fancy weapon of some kind? Expensive, I bet.'

Daimonia bit his hand furiously, her eyes as wild as a cat's. She chewed as the man screamed, grinding his flesh.

He ripped away, shaking his arm up and down as if afire. An inhuman wail loosed from his mouth.

Daimonia scrambled to her feet and shoved him with all her weight. He toppled, arms spinning, and plunged into the cesspit with a phenomenal splash. Waste spattered profusely.

Daimonia laughed.

The neighing of horses announced a patrol of city militants riding through the deep streets. She fleetingly considered approaching them but instead made use of the dark, waiting in the shadows for the horsemen to ride past. They rode in silence, a body dragging behind them, soggy and twitching.

Daimonia turned her eyes to the sky, tasting the blood on her lips with a gasp. The starry constellations felt so familiar tonight, like a song made out of light. The city was so strange and alien by comparison, a huge scab on a beautiful world. Such places built unfinished men, brick people who had no hearts. She did not belong here. Instead she was soothed by a peaceful desire to die, to surrender to Great Mother Cerenox and be the smallest part of something divine.

The Goddess did not claim Daimonia's life. Instead the girl crept through the city until the sun revealed the debris of the night, like a tide drawing back over wreckage.

She knew it was not her home, but Daimonia was drawn back to the fortress. Across the bridge the great edifice stood waiting, its courtyards already busy with the labour of smiths, farriers, porters and watchmen. Here lived the family of knights Daimonia would never be a part of. She found her way back to the squire's door and banged on it with light but hurried knocks. 'Magpie! Let me in!'

Magpie appeared in a sleeping hat and a nightgown. He frowned at the sight of her. 'What am I – some kindly idiot?' He bent away, making to escape.

Daimonia caught his sleeve. 'Please, I just need my things!'

'I'm under strict instructions not to admit you.' Magpie shook his head. 'Captain Vornir has been telling us how difficult you were to bring up. The poor lady practically gave up her life for you!'

'Oh, shut up, you idiot!' She grabbed him and pressed the tip of her dagger to his throat. 'You know nothing!'

'You make a persuasive point!' Magpie conceded. He snuck the girl through the corridor and into his own quarters. 'I don't normally entertain,' he explained as they entered a dingy room. The walls were covered with paintings of nudes of every shape and size, a fruity forest of breasts and bottoms.

'I see you enjoy art.' Daimonia folded her arms tightly.

Magpie followed her gaze. 'I get what I can,' he admitted. He quickly set his candle down before a painting of an open-legged priestess. 'Do you want to see a portrait of me as a younger man?'

'No.'

Magpie found it anyway. 'I was quite a handsome fellow, don't you think? Good chin and lots of hair.'

'That doesn't look anything like you.' Daimonia turned away. 'Is my mother home now?'

'Yes. Catherine will be resting with young master Kasamir.' Magpie squinted at the girl. 'I'm not sure it would be a good idea to disturb her. But she'll be up to organise the night patrols later. Maybe we can sort something out.'

'I don't want to talk to her.' Daimonia helped herself to an apple. 'I'll collect everything when she is gone.'

'Well, I'll pour you a bath, then. Looks like you've been to Archonia and back!'

'No need.' She took a candle and began exploring as he tailed her.

'By the way, I never married,' Magpie declared as he followed her backside. 'What with working for the knights and everything.'

Daimonia evaded the squire, feeling her way along the time-worn stone. She pursued silence, avoiding all the sounds of life until candlelight discovered the ornamental entrance to a forgotten hero-chapel.

Opening the engraved bronze door, she let herself inside. She found peace and solemnity within, as if the world had been abruptly left behind. The chapel was filled with cobwebbed debris, broken urns and scurrying rodents. She paused to relish the darkness, to let it cocoon her. *I'll live here in the dark*, she mused. *I'll haunt this chapel with ghoulish cries, and when the knights come to investigate, I'll scream!*

She laughed but then let out a yell as her flame exposed an unexpected shape. A stone knight with a decayed face emerged from the dark as if advancing to meet her. The figure was frozen in a moment of battle, shield raised, sword poised to deliver a strike.

'Good morning.' Daimonia curtsied once her heart had stopped racing. She waited for the stone to respond, and when it didn't, she grew bolder. She moved towards the antique thing, peering at its cracked visage. 'I thought you had abandoned me.' She touched the decaying face, savouring the gritty texture upon her fingers.

Daimonia poked and prodded at the thing, half-expecting it to crumble to pieces. The statue remained steadfast despite the girl's explorations. Finally she threw an arm around its enormous shoulders. 'Welcome to the Underworld,' she said, as if she had arrived first.

When there was no reply, she sat upon the statue's base and leaned against its cold legs. 'Here we are, Goodkin,' she told the stone. 'Journey's end and it has all come to nothing. What's that you say? You don't want to be drawn into my story? Too late. It has already killed us both.'

She fell to the ground as if struck by an arrow. There she lay, motionless and in silence, imitating death for as long as she was able. She fantasised about her mother finding her body. Wondered if Catherine would hate herself for not loving enough? But perhaps only someone capable of love could know regret. The truth was, the world

212

would go on without Daimonia, just as it had without Niklos. Finally she arose and turned back to the stone.

'We came looking for a vengeful Goddess that did not exist. But do you know what I have realised? We can create her anyway.'

The Screaming Stars

It was the last night of the season and the celebration of Cere-Thalatte, the Goddess in her destructive aspect. A thousand blazing torches were carried through Khorgov's smoke-choked streets, mirroring the brilliant stars above. The lights were waved with joy by the very old and young alike, celebrating the eventual return of all things to chaos.

The festival could be heard within the many-halled fortress, where Daimonia journeyed determinedly. She travelled, candle in hand, a tiny cataract in the deep darkness.

Upon reaching her mother's room, she felt a little sick, a portentous excitement tingling through her body. Inside the dark was at its thickest. No matter how many candles Daimonia lit, the chamber would not progress beyond a wary gloom.

Now her faith would truly be put to the test. From around the room she gathered armour and weapons, examining the steel with delight. This would be the flesh of the Goddess.

She stood before the shard of glass on her mother's shrine and unsheathed the Visoth dagger. Grabbing fistfuls of her long hair, she began to cut. Locks upon locks fell in clumps to the floor until the girl's hair was short and severe like her mother's.

When all was done, she stood dressed as a Knight of the Accord, as formidable as the castellan, Captain Vornir herself. She relished the burden of the armour, as if wearing her mother's skin, inhabiting her body with her own.

'Daimonia.' She spoke her own name into the darkness, but her voice was too soft and warm.

'Daimonia!' She tried again, lacing her tone with ice and contempt. It was a good approximation of the woman she had decided to become.

When mother and daughter were as one, she shattered the glass into a thousand star-like fragments and left.

She found them packed into cells beneath the fortress. The smell was atrocious, an almost visible concoction of sweat and sewage. These were the Vendicatori, the anarchists who sought to overthrow the governance of Khorgov and of all Dalibor. Those who would spit in the eye of Prince Moranion had they the chance.

Beyond the grimy bars Daimonia saw not monsters, but children of the Goddess. These were the ordinary folk of Khorgov, exceptional only for having spoken out against the Accord. Amid their ranks she saw labourers and parents, there were vagabonds and Visoth migrants. Even disavowed knights, militants and Seidhr swelled their number, hints of a nobler order that might have been. These were the people cast as traitors in a story authored by the prince's apologists.

They regarded Daimonia with distrust and hate, mistaking her for the castellan, as the militants had when she demanded admittance to the prison. She strode amid the cells, meeting the hard faces of men and the accusing stares of women. She let their hate radiate until she was sure they would destroy her.

One woman was as brawny as the strongest men, streams of sweat coating her muscles as she held the cage bars tightly. Her hair was in tight knots, like wreaths of golden corn down her back. She bore her teeth at Daimonia, warning her off like the mother of a pride of lions.

Daimonia stood before this woman's cage as she addressed the hall. 'I am not Captain Vornir,' she told them as she began to unbolt the cells. The ancient song came to mind and she used it, appealing to their faith in the Goddess. 'I am the crown of flaming stars,' she told them. 'I am the armour forged from scars.' She searched their faces, watching hostility become assent and understanding. 'I am the truth whose seed is doubt.' Voices joined her own, swelling into a tribal ceremony. 'I am the flaming sword that will never burn out!'

The Benevolent Council of Khorgov convened in the Hall of Humility. This chamber was the grandest in the fortress, supported by decorative columns that reached to a ceiling twenty-four men high. Paintings adorned the walls, depicting both the incumbent bureaucrats and their predecessors in noble poses. A table was laid with profuse food and wine to assist the councillors in their work.

The councillors themselves were the highest quality people Khorgov had to offer. Honourable Lord Nebble Guldslag owned the finest armouries in Dalibor and was one of the nation's richest men. The Esteemed Lady Mortica was well known for her eloquent speeches on the suffering of the poor and for her grand properties in Khorgov,

Kraljevic and Leechfinger. High Priest Eligendo was the leader of the Holy Cult and had never been successfully convicted of groping boys.

'These festivities mock us!' Lord Guldslag seemed to have more teeth than other men, like the mouth of a crocodile slapped onto a human face. 'What we need is a God who inspires obedience, servitude and long-suffering. Not a harlot who incites revelry and rebellion!'

The councillors, courtiers and honorary knights showed their approval with orchestrated sycophancy. They laughed and wept with Lord Guldslag, competing for the most obsequious performance.

One red-faced and portly knight seemed especially adept at bellowing servile platitudes such as 'very good, my lord' or 'quite rightly so.' He was loud enough to attract his own sycophants, who would pat the shoulders of his untarnished armour, laughing 'well said, Marshall!'

'Perhaps the time has come to outlaw Cere-Thalatte,' Lady Mortica suggested. 'Even a Goddess must heel to the Accord.'

There was a crash like falling rock. The hall door was wracked with stress and then burst to unleash a stampede of roaring men and women. Each face was afire with rage.

The prestigious chamber erupted into a wild tumult of violence, shrill screams and cries of fury, a collective expression of the Goddess. The prisoners fell upon the fleeing bureaucrats, who tried to escape in a confusion of chicken legs, spilled wine and shattered glass.

'This is an outrage!' someone was shouting. One of the council militants grabbed Daimonia, but she used his momentum to throw him face first into a trough of food. Meat and gravy splashed liberally.

Only Lord Guldslag stood his ground, commanding the rebels to desist. His face glistened as he shouted, his cheeks still wet with the oils of his sumptuous meal. He was promptly relieved of every kind of wealth and dignity and his head replaced by that of a dead pig.

Daimonia was ankle deep in blood, stepping over the bodies of militants and nobles alike. She felt neither regret nor vindication, only a growing sense of predestination.

Mother and daughter met on the bridge at dawn. The crimson sky was raked with claws of lightning.

Daimonia led out her army of traitors. Having looted the fortress armoury, these avengers were dressed and prepared for battle.

Catherine stood at the forefront of her knights, the most senior officers at the front and beyond them units of militants, men-at-arms, crossbowmen and archers.

'What new madness is this?' Catherine was shaking, her face twitching with incredulity. She stared at Daimonia as if the girl were a once-loved horse needing to be put down. Kasamir stood by her side, grinning lecherously as if his world were not about to end. The Accord officers stared fearfully, as if into the pit of Archonia.

'This is the madness of the Goddess.' Daimonia spoke with authority. 'That which was contained by force will now be set loose with equal force.'

Catherine shooed away the declaration. 'You're not a prophet, Daimonia. You're part of a problem, old as life. Fools believe we can do without law and punishment. But look at what happens when you give free rein to barbarity; your allies are condemned by the very blood on their faces.'

'Don't you see?' Daimonia insisted. 'These revolutionaries are your creation. Each was a voice silenced. Now silenced voices have been hammered into swords.'

'Look!' Catherine was exasperated. She waved her finger as if chastising a child. 'You're doing it right now!'

'Doing what?'

'Asking questions and being defiant.' Catherine nodded emphatically at her own words. 'This has always been your failing, although you have truly outdone yourself this time.'

'Perhaps you are right,' Daimonia admitted. 'All you have given me are wounds, and wounds are all I have to give.'

'You hope to commit a famous treason,' said Catherine. 'But your story threatens to corrupt the young and encourage them to celebrate the downfall of their betters. No, it must have an ending most horrid so that others do not fall into madness, as you have.'

'It seems to me that we are both mad,' Daimonia replied, 'but only I know it.'

Catherine could hardly look at her daughter. 'What would your brother make of you now?' she lamented.

'My brother is dead.' The words seemed to drip with blood as Daimonia spoke them.

Catherine's strength faltered. She staggered and fought to retain her composure, pulling her arm away from Kasamir when he tried to console her. She shrank under Daimonia's vindictive stare, as if she were now the child. With visible effort she managed to regain herself and force a reply. 'Why not you instead of him?'

A terrible heartsick cry rose from Daimonia's throat, releasing all grief in one strenuous expulsion. She unsheathed her sword and dagger, cutting and stabbing in a hail of hate.

Those who leapt forward in Catherine's defence lost bits of themselves in the furore. A knight fell to his knees, his hand spouting blood from the stump of each finger. Another lost an eye.

Catherine grabbed Daimonia's forearms and pushed back with all her armoured weight, hurling Daimonia to the floor. As the girl scraped across the ground, Catherine secured her shield and drew her Guldslag broadsword, advancing upon her daughter.

The fighters took this as a signal to attack. Daimonia's outlaws stampeded towards the knights, who met the charge with a wall of shields and heavy armour. Cruel swords gleamed and war horns bellowed as the tides of men competed.

Daimonia lifted her head from the ground. Little fragments of stone were stuck into her face. She arose amidst a tumult of grim close-quarters fighting. Blood sprayed and spattered, men slipped on the gory thoroughfare, and muscles unleashed blow after blow of bone-cracking brutality.

A knight lunged for the girl and she stabbed at his face with her dagger. His knees gave and she leapt past, burying her sword into a charging militant. She cut at two men who tried to grab her and stabbed another who had climbed onto the bridge wall; his body flopped into the moat below.

Daimonia's tongue rolled over the scar on her lips as she brandished her weapons. 'I have more wounds to inflict,' she shouted, her eyes seeking out her enemy.

Catherine fought on the edge of the bridge, stabbing round the rim of her shield. As traitors assailed her, she split them with quick precise stabs. Kasamir fought determinedly beside her, striking out with an increasingly dented blade.

Daimonia battled through the melee until she was almost behind them. She seized Kasamir's hair in her fist and slit his throat with a cackle. She opened the mouth of his wound to her mother, baptising her with arterial waste.

'Go to the Goddess,' Daimonia prayed, advancing with her blades.

Catherine hissed, her white cloak now sopping red. Rage tightened her face, revealing fangs for teeth and eyes black as Archonia's pits. Her body shook, racked by a powerful hate. 'You – are – my – curse!' The words came out in heaving breaths.

The Vornir women circled each other, leaning close enough to hug. There was a flash in the sky and they struck, blades wedged into each other's flesh. Catherine rolled her head at the sky, groaning as if in labour before she forced Daimonia back with a powerful kick.

Daimonia fell into the struggling fighters. For a moment she was overwhelmed by the reek of sweat and injury. These warriors were her brothers and sisters now, their faces bone white as another claw of lightning ripped the sky. She launched herself from their battle and swung at Catherine with all her force.

Catherine blocked, turning the blow away with her embossed shield. She swept her own blade up and struck Daimonia's hand. The girl's sword spun, reflecting the storm, and was lost. With a piercing cry, Catherine swung for Daimonia's neck. Thunder shook the sky.

Daimonia rolled under the attack, evading with a performer's grace. She lunged, her dagger gashing the face she had longed to touch. *Sacrilege*, her heart responded, but she was beyond repentance.

Catherine's dark brows oozed blood. Half-blind, she retaliated, sweeping high and low. Her sword was vicious and quick, but the girl was already behind her.

Daimonia grabbed her mother's cloak, making a fist in the bloodstained cloth. She wrenched hard, pulling Catherine into her arms, and then stabbed her in the breast. The Visoth dagger tasted flesh beneath armour. 'I cannot find your heart,' Daimonia mocked.

Catherine wailed and span free, bashing Daimonia's skull with her shield. She seethed, spitting curses, as the girl stumbled amid the growing mounds of corpses. 'You can never win, you evil girl!'

Daimonia felt the world spin. Blood streamed from her scalp like the caress of warm fingers. It seeped down her neck and trickled beneath her armour, becoming intimate with her burning skin. She was knocked back through the melee, as if gliding from suitor to suitor at a ball. Conflict encircled her as she became the eye of a violent whirlwind – the fulcrum of destruction.

Her mother was charging, her red-white cloak raised like seraphic wings. Daimonia grabbed a spear from the dying and hurled it haphazardly, killing some other foe. She threw an axe, a helm and a

222

dagger. Each met Catherine's shield. Finally Daimonia pulled a broadsword from the stomach of a corpse and set loose.

Passion possessed mother and daughter as they sliced at each other. Faces twisted in fury, they fought in agony of body and spirit. When they broke apart, Daimonia was wreathed in the blood of them both. Her face was ugly with emotions too turbulent to give name to.

'I see it.' Catherine laughed between tears. She was bleeding from a dozen vengeful cuts, crouched over her shield as she shivered. 'Even now you want love.'

'You are incapable of giving it.'

An arrow arced over the carnage and penetrated Catherine's throat. Her eyes bulged and she dribbled a ripple of blood down her neck and armour.

Daimonia went to hold her, but Catherine was backing away, warding her off. The girl watched helplessly as her mother fell to one knee and then the other. Their eyes met, but with confusion and pain rather than understanding. Catherine looked surprised by the cruelty of the world – it was an expression so typical of poor Niklos. Then she was dead.

Daimonia dropped to the ground and threw her arms around her mother. She shifted the armoured corpse so it seemed they held each other. She hugged the cold body as all around turned to chaos.

A shout rose among all the combatants, one voice quickly becoming many. The fortress had erupted in flame, the inferno illuminating the ferocious conflict. This was an act that would be swiftly answered by burnings throughout Khorgov. A sign the revolution had begun. The word would spread from city to city, wrath poured from beacon to fiery beacon.

Daimonia rose in the blistering firestorm heat. She was the torch that had ignited this conflagration. As the highest turrets crumbled, a crown of light lit the sky, a diadem of flaming stones. She basked in the terrible glow, savouring her brilliant coronation.

Now she knew with absolute certainty. She was the Goddess of War. She was the avenger, chaos and death. She was Cere-Thalatte and the falling stars were a measure of her anger.

As the heavenly fire descended, she raised her sword, light flashing on the bloody tip. Shadows took life and prowled the battleground, delineating the abundant dead. The Goddess had repaid greed with slaughter, a thousand lives shed for one.

As the screaming stars rained down, her laughter became a haunting song.

I am the crown of eternal stars,
I am the armour forged from scars,
I am the truth whose seed is doubt,
I am the flaming sword that will never burn out!

APPENDICES

THE CAST

The Vornir Family

Daimonia Vornir – A questioning young woman

Niklos Vornir – Daimonia's brother, a Knight of the Accord

Jhonan Vornir – Daimonia's grandfather, a retired Accord Knight

Catherine Vornir – Daimonia's mother, castellan of Khorgov Fortress

The Geld Knight and his Enforcers

Sir Conrad Ernst – A Geld Knight and former apologist

Fotter – A trapper and animal molester

Scorcher – An arsonist and delinquent

The Afreyan – A mysterious swordsman

Cain – 400 lb of muscle

The Way Knight and his Passengers

Goodkin – A Way Knight

Hem – A simple boy from Littlecrook

Purtur – A travelling merchant, Hem's father

Svek – A wrinkled Seidhr courier and pervert

Fletcher, Isolde and Pickle – Refugees from Chalkwater

Nobles, Politicians and other Criminals

Baron Volk Leechfinger – The ruler of Leechfinger

Pavel – An apologist, Conrad's mentor

The Duke of Knave – The ruler of Knave and cousin to the prince

Dobra Knave – The duke's daughter

Lord Nebble Guldslag – Chairman of the Council of Khorgov

Prince Moranion – The ruler of Dalibor and master of the Accord

John Grobian – A former Accord mercenary, now an outlaw

Astur – Proprietor of a brothel

Dreja – A prisoner of Astur

The Triple Goddess and other Gods

Ceresoph – Divine curiosity and creation

Cerenox – Maternal Love

Cere-Thalatte – Chaos, Destruction and War

Chrestos – The brother of the Goddess, all that is best in men

Gorach Baoth, the Burning Man – The god of the Baoth

Rakasha – A universal spirit worshipped by the Urothians

Questions for Reading Groups and Students

'A good question is better than a poor answer.'

I know that reading groups enjoy chewing over books and that some students may read *The Way Knight*. I offer the following questions as potentially useful.

About the characters and story

1) Is Daimonia the hero or the villain of *The Way Knight?*

2) Daimonia's father is not directly mentioned in the story. What assumptions might we make about him?

3) What thoughts do you imagine Goodkin had about Daimonia? Was she just another 'passenger'?

4) What happens next for Sir Conrad Ernst the Geld Knight?

5) Why might Catherine have abandoned her children?

6) What has happened at the end? Is Daimonia divine or is she deluded? Is it the end of the world or the beginning of a new age?

Social and philosophical themes

1) What words would be used to describe Daimonia if she were a person in the modern world?

2) What frustrations might lead a person to become disaffected with society or opposed to the state?

3) How damaging is corruption at the top?

4) What is one thing that would make for a better, fairer society?

5) What, if anything, is the relationship between power and virtue?

6) What, if anything, is the relationship between certainty and truth?

Acknowledgements

'Who would attempt that journey for the sake of a story?'

Special thanks to my team of Way Knights. Thanks to Adele for being my Goodkin, for giving me firm advice and being there each step of the way. Love to Rebecca for being my Daimonia, questioning everything! Cheers to Akasha, for your boundless enthusiasm when you have so many of your own talents to express. Heroic salutes to Sarah, for always being a steadfast ally.

All hail the artists! Phil – thanks for coming on another adventure with me. Through the caves and ruins of our imaginations and onto the page! Thank you, Anastasia, for bringing your special gift to the characters of The Way Knight. It's been a pleasure working with you both.

Thanks to Pauline, Ben and Fay for your excellent support.

Thanks to Gilly, for hosting those cosy readings. Warriors huddled around a candle, with nothing but wine and port to fend off the shadows.

Waves and gratitude to Chris, Jeremy, Jane, Dan and all the wonderful people at CHINDI.

For a **free story**, set in the world of **THE WAY KNIGHT,**

please email:

thewayknight@outlook.com

Alexander Wallis graduated from the University of Chichester, where he studied Youth and Community Work. Thousands of young people have benefited from his well-being workshop *Are You Mental?* Alexander's novel, *The Way Knight*, was inspired by the struggles faced by young people growing up in dysfunctional families, systems and societies. You can follow his writing online via: www.facebook.com/AlexanderWallisAuthor

Phil Ives achieved his master's degree in Fine Art, Illustration at Aberystwyth University. He enjoys adapting his art to meet different requirements and likes to bridge the gap between traditional and digital techniques. He now lives in Staffordshire and works as a freelance illustrator and painter. For commission inquiries, Phil can be contacted at phil.a.ives@hotmail.co.uk

Anastasia Ilecheva is a Russian illustrator whose portfolio appears on DeviantArt under the name Entreprenurial. Anastasia is a student of architecture and design, who has been inspired by 19th and 20th century Russian artists. Anastasia welcomes enquiries about commissions via: lolipoppa@mail.ru